Potomac Review

Published by the Paul Peck Humanities Institute at
Montgomery College, Rockville
51 Mannakee Street, Rockville, MD 20850

Potomac Review has been made possible through
the generosity of Montgomery College.

A special thanks to Dean Rodney Redmond.

For submission guidelines and more information:
http://potomacreview.org

Potomac Review, Inc. is a not-for-profit 501 c(3) corp.
Member, Council of Literary Magazines & Presses
Indexed by the American Humanities Index
ISBN: 978-0-9889493-8-6
ISSN 10073 – 1989

SUBSCRIBE TO *POTOMAC REVIEW*
One year at $24 (2 issues)
Two years at $36 (4 issues)
Sample copy order, $10 (Single issue)

Design by Carol Chu
Cover photo by John L. Hoover

TABLE OF CONTENTS

ANOTHER SONG IN THE DESERT

CHAD SCHUSTER

You have to buy the right cut of meat, first of all. Heritage breed, or at least something organic. Then you have to brine it. Water, sugar, salt, in exactly the right proportions. Then you have to cook it to the perfect temperature, 145 degrees, just barely above of what's safe to eat. If you do not do these things, if you fail to take even one of these steps, the pork will be dry. And the pork must not be dry. If the pork is dry, Tom will be insufferable. He will come home from his construction trailer, the same place he has worked for forty years, and he will react in one of two ways. One possibility is that he will sulk. He will not say anything about the pork being dry, but he will become very quiet, even quieter than usual, and as he eats the pork he will make faces that indicate extreme displeasure. The other possibility, and this one is more likely, is that Tom will be overtly upset about the dryness of the pork. He might even refuse to eat it, opting instead to order pizza or takeout and deduct the cost of his replacement meal from Violet's weekly allowance.

This occurred on Christmas one year, not with pork, but with pot roast, and because no one was delivering pizza on Christmas, Tom drove to the mini-mart down the street to purchase nachos, the quality of which he complained about, but he ate them anyway, out of principle, and charged Violet a penalty fee of twenty-five dollars in addition to the nominal cost of the replacement meal.

Chrissy, Tom and Violet's only child, used to defend Violet on these occasions. Tom had no interest in leniency, he generally ignored Chrissy, but it was nonetheless of great consolation to Violet to have someone else in the room to see the spectacle and validate her unstated position that Tom was, at the very least, a difficult man. Now that Chrissy was gone, suicide, last Thanksgiving, Violet was very much alone. So what else was there to do but cook the pork, following the protocol she had developed decades ago, in addition to executing similar protocols she had developed for other household chores, dishes, laundry, grocery shopping and such? She lived her days ever vigilant, ever conscious of Tom's moods.

She could have married someone else, perhaps. She could have insisted she learn how to drive. That would have made more sense. But everything substantial in her life happened when she was very young, just a girl, really, so that when she looked back as an oldish woman it seemed the important decisions she had made, the ones that had shaped the course of her life, were not really made by her. They were made by a different Violet, a girl who read poetry, Rilke, Kipling, Whitman, and mistook Tom's temper for strength. And now the current Violet, the one who still read poetry but had since come to see Tom as nothing more than a bully—she was the one left to suffer the consequences. But not anymore.

There had been that brilliant moment eight months ago that set her escape in motion. It started with a question that came to her from nowhere, turning an ordinary pork night into something else. She was at the grocery store weighing potatoes, four of them in a bag. She looked at their skin, cratered and soiled. Such ugly things. She set the bag on the metal scale and watched the red needle tremble into place. She wrote down the weight on her notepad as she always did, doing the math longhand for price verification later at the register. And then it hit her, the kind of inwardly focused question that causes all uprisings: How is it possible to not know the weight of your own unhappiness? She stood breathless in the produce section, marveling at the question's simplicity. How did she not know? After dinner that night she called Gloria and told her she was ready to leave Tom.

"Only you can make a decision like this, dear," Gloria said. "I'm here for you either way."

Now, after months of planning, Violet had a recipe card printed on ordinary paper, the same kind she and Gloria had been emailing back and forth for two years. It was like all the others, except this one had the word "Freedom" listed as the title of the dish. It had three very easy to follow instructions:

Pack a suitcase

Take a bus to the airport

Fly to the desert to live with Gloria

For her final meal with Tom, Violet cooked pork, dry, the consistency of a well-worn shoe. She sat at the dinner table and watched his face contort as he ate and she felt very good, as happy as she had felt in a long time. "I'm not sure what you mean, darling," she said. "This tastes fine to me." Tom looked at her as if she had just bombed an orphanage. It took tremendous effort for her not to laugh.

The next morning, Tom left for work at dawn, same as always. Violet had written a note. She had folded the note and slipped it into an envelope. She had sealed the envelope and written Tom's name on the outside. Now she held the envelope in her hands. She pressed it against her chest and closed her eyes. Then she set it on the dining room table where she knew he would find it. She pulled the recipe card from her purse and read it again, for courage. Then she took one last look at her home, the place she had spent most of her adult life. It had already lost its power over her. Looking around, she saw the spot near the bay window where Chrissy took her first steps, the place in the corner where they put the Christmas tree each year. She saw the couch where Tom had once raped her, she was certain now that rape is what had happened that night, rape, that is the absolute right thing to call it, and she lamented again that she didn't do this years ago. She walked to the end table and picked up a framed photo of Chrissy in grade school during what was, in hindsight, the happiest time in her life. Violet looked at the photo for a moment. She felt her chest rising and falling. No tears, no tears. And, thankfully, there were none. She unzipped her suitcase and put the photo inside. Then she walked out the door and into the world. It was a Tuesday.

The sun was blinding, brilliant, already heating a September morning that looked and felt nothing like early autumn. There were birds, flowers. A lawnmower wailed in the distance. She was nearly to the corner when she saw Mrs. Wells and her yippy little dog walking toward her.

"Good morning, Mrs. Wells!" Violet knew she sounded too excited. She softened her voice. "Lovely day, isn't it?"

"It is lovely," Mrs. Wells said, looking down at the ancient suitcase Violet was dragging behind her. "I hope you're headed somewhere fun."

"Just leaving for a few days to visit a friend," Violet said. "In Alberta." Alberta? Where had that come from? She couldn't locate Alberta on a map and yet somehow it was the first place that popped into her head. "An old friend of mine married a Canadian," she continued, becoming increasingly impressed by the elaborateness of her lie. "She's been begging me for years to go up there. Now's my chance."

"That sounds nice," Mrs. Wells said. "We'll be sure to look after Tom while you're away." She winked.

Violet tried to relax. "Please do," she said, laughing. "Someone will have to."

It was only five blocks to the bus stop, but by the time Violet made it there she was exhausted. Paranoia was setting in, guilt was setting in. What if Tom came home early? What if he rolled by in his big white truck and saw her sitting at the bus stop, clutching the handle of their suitcase? Then she remembered: Tom would not come home early. When Chrissy was a little girl, she would play with her dolls all morning, but by late afternoon she was making frequent trips to the window to look for his truck. She spent too many hours waiting for that man, watching the sky darken. Ten minutes, twenty minutes. Thirty. The bus was late. Something was wrong. She walked to the mini-mart and used the payphone to call the transit hotline. Mechanical problems. Service on her route was running an hour behind. She went back to the bus stop to wait.

When she got to the bank, she went straight to the ladies' room and splashed water on her face, carefully, to avoid ruining her mascara. She was wearing her favorite blouse, white with purple flowers. Violets. She knew it was silly to wear a shirt with such an obvious connection to her name, but it made her bolder somehow, more herself. "You can do this, Violet," she said aloud to the mirror. She walked back into the sterile light of the bank. She was fourth in line. The middle-aged man in front of her was chatting with a woman not much older than Chrissy.

"I heard it on the radio in the car just now," the woman said. "They said it was a plane."

"Huh," the man said. "That doesn't sound good."

Violet was sweating. She could feel her heart beating in her wrist, her neck. It was beating everywhere. "Can I help you with anything else?" said the woman behind the glass, smiling brightly as she handed Violet a massive wad of cash. So much, Violet thought. So, so much. "No, thank you," she said.

The airport was throbbing with activity. It had been nearly ten years since Violet last flew on an airplane, a company trip to Hawaii during which Tom refused to wear shorts despite eighty degree temperatures, and spent most of his time complaining or wandering the vast open-air hallways of the hotel. The terminal hadn't changed much. She remembered the restlessness of the place, the cumulative hum of distracted energy, thousands of people on a mission to be somewhere else. But despite the illusion of activity, no one seemed to be moving. A crowd was gathered around a television in a waiting area. Violet wheeled her suitcase up to the mass of people. She tapped the woman in front of her on the shoulder.

"Excuse me," Violet said. "Do you know what's going on?"

The woman had thin colorless lips and blue bags under her eyes. She looked at Violet incredulously. "Haven't you seen the news?"

Violet had not seen the news. She had spent all morning worrying, fleeing. "No," she said. "I haven't."

"We're under attack," the woman said. "Someone is crashing planes into buildings. They've hit New York and they just hit Washington."

Violet found a payphone and called Gloria. "Are you seeing this?" Violet asked. "Are you watching this?"

"Of course," Gloria said. "I think the whole planet is watching."

"I don't know how I'm going to get down there," Violet said. She started to say something else, then stopped herself.

"Are you still coming?" Gloria said. "I hate to say this, but you could go home to Tom. He would never know the difference."

Violet was silent for a long time. She looked across the terminal toward the people watching television. She thought of the note sealed in an envelope on the dining room table.

"I'm not going home," she said. "I can't go back."

Violet spent two nights in a hotel near the airport. After much trying she secured a seat on a bus next to an old man who smelled of burnt tobacco. He was the kind of ancient Southerner whose skin seems likely to tear in a high wind. Each of his heavy breaths was a deliberate act of self-preservation. This annoyed Violet at first. She felt responsible for tracking his breathing when all she wanted to do was rest. A hundred miles later the breathing had become a source of comfort, something to rely on. She could peripherally see the pearl buttons on the man's checkered shirt rising and falling in rhythm. She counted the breaths, one to a hundred, then started over, the country gliding by outside the window, the soft chatter of other passengers blending nicely with the churnings and rattlings of the bus, its interior smelling of plastic and some kind of ethnic food someone was eating nearby.

The man had been asleep for a good hour, his lungs processing air in a pattern that Violet had come to trust, when suddenly his breathing stopped. Violet waited a moment. Her heartbeat quickened, her own breaths came faster. She felt herself sweating despite the cold wind being generated by the air conditioner. She stirred in her seat, hoping it would rouse him. Nothing. She stirred harder. She rummaged through her purse, snapping buttons, opening and closing zippers loudly, but the man's breathing did not return. She looked around. No one was paying any attention. She was on the verge of screaming when the man started breathing again, his chest sputtering for a moment before falling back into its normal pattern.

"It was horrifying, Gloria." Violet was at a rest stop payphone, the bus glinting in the sun behind her. "I could have sworn he was dead." Heat shimmered above the parking lot. The sun was evil, a powerful force bent on destruction.

"That sounds awful," Gloria said. "You poor thing. I really can't wait to see you, Violet. All this time as friends, never once having the pleasure of meeting in person. With all that's going on right now, it's hard to be alone. I give great foot rubs, you know. You'll see."

The bus rolled westward. Violet and the breathing man shared the kind of silence that becomes an understanding, a benevolent refusal to connect. North Carolina, Tennessee, Arkansas. American skies flew by, all of them different but connected, like lines in an old poem tumbling down the page. Flags. How many of them did she see? Flapping on poles, strung up in windows, catching breezes on gulf-facing porches. The immensity of Texas, the audacity of it. She had seen it on the map her whole life, so self-assured sitting there at the bottom of the country, propping the rest of the states up. Now here it was up close. Tom had never been to Texas. Tom could not handle Texas. But here was Violet, handling it, slicing through its heart on a silver bus, reminding herself again that she should have done this years ago.

It was Friday. She was three days into her new life, a woman, sixty-six years old and alone. She had good skin still and a trusting smile. She was thin, she had always eaten well and made sure to watch her figure. Eventually she would settle finances with Tom and they would both move on. Finally, it was her time. Looking out the window at some dusty Texas town she saw two men in cowboy hats talking in front of a gas station. She saw a man with a determined face propelling his wheelchair down the sidewalk, a cluster of kids running across brown grass in the midday heat. She saw these things and felt so much joy in her chest that she feared she would explode. She had gained extra senses, it seemed. She could feel the blood rushing through her veins. She could read faces, see thoughts. Tom, Chrissy, the terrorists—everyone made sense. She understood. She did not forgive, but she understood. She counted the breaths of the man next to her. She was in the forties when the breathing stopped. This time she was prepared.

It wouldn't be long before his chest started moving again.

Except it didn't. She began counting the breaths that weren't there. Again she became restless, her heart thumped, she was falling into the same trap as last time. She decided to hold out. She tried looking out the window but her attention kept returning to the motionless pearl buttons on the man's flannel shirt. She nudged him softly, waited. She nudged again, slightly harder. Then a third time, this time angrily, with more force than she had intended. She began shaking him violently, trying to jar him back to life.

"Sir! Sir!" She was yelling now, fully consumed by panic, people in nearby seats looking at her like she was crazy. "Sir!"

He opened his eyes, startled. She was an idiot. She knew this now. What was she doing here on this bus, slashing through Texas, startling this poor man half to death? "I'm so sorry," she said. "You stopped breathing."

The man smiled sheepishly. He was missing teeth. He shrugged. "Sleep apnea," he said. A hundred miles later the man got off in some God-awful outpost called Lordsburg.

You reach a point where you can't undo things. Violet had reminded herself of this many times before, when she overcooked meat, say, or spilled cranberry juice on the white linen tablecloth and there was nothing to do but stand there frowning with her arms at her side, watching the red liquid bleed across the fabric. So it was now, in Arizona, with the sun climbing into the sky behind a scorched mountain, that she thought to herself again: I cannot go back. Soon she would be at her friend's little slice of heaven. That's how Gloria had always referred to her home on the recipe sharing website where they first met, and later on the phone after they'd struck up a friendship and came to realize all the things they had in common.

Gloria had been married too, for nearly thirty years, to a

man who sold heavy machinery, tractors or something, the kind of job that required him to buy steak dinners for gruff men in sturdy, out of the way cities. Billings, Butte, Jackson Hole. He flew off and left Gloria alone to cook and sew and go to book club. It was fine, it was good, really, Gloria made it a point to say this to Violet each time they talked about the shortcomings of their husbands. Joe, God rest his soul, had tried. But all Gloria really wanted was a partner, someone to talk to and go on walks with. She didn't need all the money he was making, which turned out to be a good thing since Joe managed to squander nearly everything before he died standing knee-deep in a Wyoming river, a heart attack during a fishing trip with a client. He didn't drink or gamble. This was an important point. He was not out there selfishly satisfying his lowest cravings. What he did was he invested, badly, one failed venture after another. Energy in the eighties, technology in the nineties. Not the wrong sectors but the wrong companies. It was just a matter of bad luck.

"This is why I live in a mobile home," Gloria said, laughing, as she and Violet drove away from the bus station. "If just one of those companies had hit we'd have been rich. Least that's the way Joe always put it." Gloria was thick everywhere and had coarse white hair that shot straight toward the desert sun. She had Old Glory pinned to the breast of her white sweater, on which a scowling eagle was superimposed over another flapping flag. She wore large black sunglasses that made it impossible to see her eyes. They were driving through a sea of mobile homes, hundreds of them arranged along a winding road at the foot of a mountain outside Tucson. The homes were small, bordering on trailers, much smaller than the one Violet had shared with Tom, but the yards were well kept and the people sitting on their porches in plastic chairs smiled when you went by. Every single home displayed a flag. Gloria drove by the swimming pool at the center of the community, pointing out Rudy and

Elizabeth, Roy and Irene, along with others Violet couldn't keep track of, a collection of tanned shriveled bodies moving through the blue water. Gloria stopped the car near the chain link fence.

"Hi Reenie!" She yelled through the open car window. A plump woman in goggles and a purple bathing suit was poised on the edge of a diving board. She remained in diving posture but turned her head toward the car, delivering a stern-faced nod before plunging head first into the pool. They continued down the road past a man in huge white tennis shoes, shuffling behind a walker. The walker had tennis balls covering each of its four legs. The man smiled at them as they rolled by.

"Howdy Chuck," Gloria said through the window, and the man nodded back.

"Seems like you have a lot of friends here," Violet said.

"Acquaintances," Gloria said. "You never really know that many people well enough to call them friends. Chuck lives next door. He's harmless."

The car came to rest in front of powder blue mobile home. They sat for a moment listening to the ticks beneath the hood. A sign planted in the garden said "Heaven" with an arrow pointing toward the front door.

"Welcome home," Gloria said, and she opened the car door, ushering in a blast of heat that nearly knocked Violet out of her seat. The interior of Gloria's home was all mahogany. There were wood panels on the walls and ceiling, accented by pink and orange and yellow paint. It was like living inside a desert sunset, Gloria said. "You have to understand," she explained. "Before this I spent twelve years in Alberta." She crossed her arms over her chest and pretended to shiver. "Imagine a southern belle like me banished to the great white north. It's freezing up there. This sun saved my life."

"You lived in Alberta?" Violet said. "How do I not know that?"

Gloria smiled. "Oh dear," she said. "There must be so many things we don't know about each other. Luckily we have all kinds of time to tease them out." She winked. They sat for a while talking, and later they shared a quiet dinner, roast chicken, rice pilaf, asparagus, a bottle of chardonnay. They talked about Violet's trip across the country, how she was feeling about things, and about the people in the towers, those poor, poor people, the courage of the ones who rushed in to save others and the ones who chose to jump rather than give themselves up to the flames. When it was time for bed, Gloria showed Violet to her room. It was immaculate. The linen on the bed, which took up most of the room, looked like it had been turned down by a professional.

The night was colder than Violet expected. She pulled the blankets all the way up under her chin and stared into the dark. The air conditioner was deafening. It rustled the sheer curtains, moonlight seeping through, and the little paper lanterns Gloria had hung around the perimeter of the room, causing them to tap softly against the wall. Violet turned on the lamp and sat up. She got out of bed and went to her suitcase. She unzipped the outside pocket and removed the picture of Chrissy. She walked over to the dresser and cleared a space between the dozen or so stuff animals Gloria had standing watch on its surface. She used her nightgown to wipe clean the glass in the picture frame, and she looked at the picture, her sweet little girl, for a long time. Then she set the picture down on the dresser, returned to bed and clicked off the lamp.

Two hours later she woke up. The moon was gone and the room was completely black. Rain the size of pork chops was clanging off the tin roof. She sat up in bed, listening. Then she got up and opened the window. It was still hot outside. She watched the rain fall, little rivers swelling at the edge of the street, until she knew without question she wouldn't be able to go back to sleep. It was after midnight when she tiptoed toward the kitchen to make a cup of tea. She was expecting an empty room but there was Gloria, sitting in her nightgown at the glass table, flipping through a magazine. She smiled at Violet.

"Can't sleep, huh?"

"No," Violet said. "Just a little wound up, I guess."

"Well, I confess," Gloria said. "I'm an insomniac. I look through these terrible tabloids hoping they'll put me to sleep. Course these days they're much easier to read than the real news."

"Yes," Violet whispered. "All of this is hard to take." She stood there a moment, not sure what to do next. Then she started crying, at first softly and then with a force that surprised her.

Gloria hustled over to offer her a hug. "There, there," she said. "You've sure been through a lot." She squeezed tightly and Violet squeezed back because she needed to feel close to someone. Gloria began rubbing Violet's back gently, in tiny little circles, and Violet thought it felt nice but a part of her also wondered what exactly Gloria was trying to communicate with the back rubbing. Then Gloria took Violet's face in her rough hands. She looked her straight in the eye and smiled a sad smile. She wiped away one of Violet's tears with the back of her knuckle, and Violet closed her eyes and tilted her head toward the floor, just for a moment, long enough to gather herself, and when she looked back up she could barely see through the tears but she could see well enough to know that Gloria's expression had changed. It was a look she had not seen from anyone in years, decades, but one she understood well, the kind of look that no one ever forgets no matter how long it's been. The kind of look that brought with it another important question: When you are a mature woman with traditional values and an equally mature woman with equally traditional values kisses you on the mouth, with tongue, what do you do?

You kiss back.

Even if you are not sure what to do, you kiss back. Because it is terrifying. Because it does not make sense. Or does it? Is this not what Violet wanted all along? It mustn't go beyond this, though. Surely there can be nothing more than kissing. But still, kiss back.

This is what Violet decided because Chrissy was in heaven and now so was Violet, sort of. She wasn't certain but this was maybe the thing she had longed for her whole life and never understood, her first taste of freedom. Tom could go fuck himself because he was at home alone sleeping or eating takeout like he deserved. Outside the rain had stopped suddenly and the clouds had parted. The stars were out. The moon was hiding behind a jagged peak and the desert was the most happening place on Earth, the canyon walls echoing with more sounds than you could imagine. Almost no one realizes how full of life the desert is in the deadliest hours of night. Wiry critters dart through the brush, lizards skitter across rain-washed roofs. Bug zappers crackle on porches. Down the street the breeze rippled the surface of the empty pool and stirred the rows of flags, each one in turn on its way to somewhere else while Chuck from next door slept upright in a recliner in front of the television, sound blaring, blue light flashing on his ghastly face, his eyes and cheeks sunken, the opposite kind of old from Violet, who at sixty-six was still very much alive, albeit paralyzed in the clutches of large semi-Canadian arms, kissing a girl for the very first time, singing "God Bless America" in her head for reasons she couldn't quite explain, or so she thought until she realized the song was not in her head at all, it was coming through the open window from Chuck's television, it was just good old Ray Charles singing America, sweet America, God done shed his grace on thee into a desert night that would not soon end.

JE SUIS PERSONNE

Barbara Siegel Carlson

Under all the wet ashes there's an abyss. No one
can take that away. Touch who I am underneath—
the blue eye of a flame. They say blue
is the fugitive color. While the coals of autumn clouds fall away
and leaves under their satin green. Under them wild earth thrives,
the dirt shines too, its powerful dust
the only smell that brings a soul to the earth.
I have never seen what's inside
of myself, in the sockets and tissues, my crannies.
My own gaping hole in the middle, my pumping
out the blood, where there's a strange rush—
a rough, raw sentiment. My pupils lure me
into the mirror of my own becoming
when no one is looking. That's how the sky gets inside.
The quivering crackle away. When I say *Je suis personne*,
it means *I am no body* like Emily D. proclaimed.
A voice that travels. A tune that begins with silence
and plays to the moon, fueled through the fibers and
filaments, blessed by the dark light of matter. I've given birth
to my own nothingness. The new nothing, virtual essence
kinetically connected. As the mute and the meek held captive
grow strong by eating dirt when they're young.
Where worms tunnel through leaving passages
that open further. Whisper in a monotone across light years.
Bodies and bones are knit to crumble
with a holy thread, the liquid emblazed

from the infinite within—it's the hottest place that knows
no earth. Through breaking we find the unbroken.

FIRE, FIRE

SHERRI H. HOFFMAN

We heard *Fire! Fire!* and hauled out of our beds like it was a
real emergency. Went pounding out the back door in our
shorts and bare feet, Ranger barking. Michael dragging his
blanket. The night sky was bright with stars, the darkness
chilly on our sleepy skins dragged from the tumble of blankets
and sheets. As soon as I figured it was Lenny, I knew we'd been
duped. Pops' Smokey Bear truck wasn't in the driveway, and
Ma was still in Indiana with her own secrets. She'd said she
needed some real Indiana warm, even though I suspected it
was something else.

Lenny must have waited until we were all asleep. That dirty
guy. There was a time I wanted to be like him. More than
that—I wanted to be him. He used to could slide a breaking
ball in under the smartest batter. Coax a rise out of a sweet
cutthroat on the Snoqualmie. Grease back a Black Ghost.
Back when we were little, and he was still a god to us.

The deadbolt had slammed behind us. Michael and David
banged on the door and Sawyer was prying at the screen on
the big window. I figured Lenny was probably not behind the
door. Most likely, he was chasing up a stash of Pops' whiskey.
Hidden between the books in the study. In a boot at the back
of a closet. They were everywhere. One time the toilet handle
broke, and when I lifted the porcelain top to secure the little
chain to the float, there was a bottle right there in the tank,

half-full of amber whiskey kept cool in the running toilet water.

I went around the side where the kitchen windows were open for the cats and rolled in under the gingham curtains. Inside, it smelled like home. Garlic and day-old bread. Sour hamster cage. Towels on the floor. Dried mud. Dog hair. Feet.

David and Michael were still hollering to let them in, but I blocked them out, listening for Lenny. I was leery of an ambush. The tinkling of metal like small bells came from Pops' bedroom, and I crept down the hallway.

Used to be summers were about catching salamanders and tadpoles in the swamp at the bottom of our road, a stolen clove cigarette behind the garage, baseball, or the horses across the way—their legs stiff with mud, muzzles like rose petals. That time the fat brown mare with the choppy mane rolled a white eye at Ranger, grabbed him in her square teeth by the scruff and tossed him over the rail. Tamped her hoof. *Out of here, dog.* The herd spun like a flock of birds turns in the sky, as if by some covert signal, bucking across the pasture, ass and tails, mud flying, farts bouncing out of the brown mare as if it was some big rehearsed joke.

That was the summer Michael was born and they didn't bring him home from the hospital for a whole month, his brain swollen with fluid. Lenny, David, and I were left by ourselves to stay up late, eat cheese sandwiches and Ovaltine, talk about what if we were orphans or which of the *Magnificent Seven* was the coolest. We ate cereal in front of the TV and watched cartoons and a double episode of *Creature Feature— Hound of the Baskervilles* and *The Blob*. Everything gave me nightmares. I must have been 5. That was the time we looked to Lenny, eager to follow him. Not anymore.

In the closet of Pops' room, a neat row of Forest Service shirts hung in a row. The chain hanging down from the ceiling fixture ticked against the bare bulb.

In the dark, I felt my way down the hall. The orange tabby, Kitty Russell, hissed from Mom's rocker. I hissed back. Chicken-shit cat. Outside the T.V. room, I let my eyes adjust. Pops called this the Rumpus Room. *'Cause you boys sure do make a rumpus.* It used to be funny. The television stations were signing off, home-of-the-brave and Apollo 17 mission video. In the flickering static, Lenny was stretched out on the couch, boots kicked up on the coffee table. He threw back another slug of whiskey straight from the bottle. The anthem peaked, and then a single note toned over the color bars on the screen. The bottle slid from Lenny's fingers to the couch, leaned up against Lenny's hip like an old friend sleeping. Lenny's eyelids drooped, closed, his breathing slowed. He looked different. Older. As if he was a stranger. As if I never knew him at all.

AGAINST COMMOTION

Ruth Foley

You are the monkey's paw—if I knew
what I had asked for, I would have held
my tongue. You are the ancient curse,
and I am living in interesting times.
If you had a mouth, I would lift my finger
to your lips, a gentle pressing. I would
quell you against my throat. In my smallest
hours, I know that I have called for you.
I know that I have wanted nothing more
than your absence. Relentless babble,
precious clang, dear radio turned up against
the hum of the highway, I wish I could hold
a morsel of your recklessness. I wish I could
let it go. I am begging now: release me
to the sinking. Press your palms hard
against my ears. Teach me to sing.

DEAR EARTH

Ruth Foley

You win. My hands are cracked
with you. My shoulders sink

beneath you. My hair is thick
with you, my eyelids weighed

with you, my mouth full.
My lungs burn with you, my legs

bend from your weight, fall
into you. I have given you

my people, given flowers and
fruit back to you, offered up

to you one waterlogged shoe
I could not afford to replace

or go without. I have prayed
for you to take me in

while you froze underneath
my back. I have let you

hold me while I watched
the sky refuse to move.

I have waited for you
to shift and open, waited

for you to release the trees.
Release the houses and

the train tracks, release
the ferns and towers. Release

the office buildings, the libraries,
the streetlamps. The late summer

flowers. The sunken lawns.
Release the stumbling mourner,

the grief-stricken. Uncle,
I said. I give, I said. You win.

A CINNABON AT MONDAWMIN

JACOB WEBER

Miss Kovac,

I need you to clean this up for me so it doesn't sound too ratchet. You made us read those two stories by kids from the hood who write the way we talk, but I couldn't get into them. I mean, I get that you want us to see ourselves in the stories we read, but I already know what I sound like. I know the problems I face. What I need to be reading are stories from people who don't have the problems I have. They must know something I don't.

So when I said "I didn't like that shit" just now, change that to whatever the right way to say it is. And take out all the places where I say "nigga." I don't really mind it, but I know you do. The first time I thought you were maybe alright was when you cried because we all called each other that. I mean, it was kind of dumb, because everyone knows us young black men call each other "nigga" all day long, and we don't mean anything by it. But you didn't want us to say that word, said it was a mean word and you left where you were from to come here because you didn't like people who said it. So I knew you were alright, even if you were a little simple.

So make this read the way it reads when you get done with your red pen in my journal. Make it sound the way people in Howard County where you live talk. Those are the people who don't have problems like the ones I have. I don't care if it's that thing you told us about the other day—appropriation. You said that was a fancy word for stealing, and there's nothing I have I wouldn't gladly let someone steal from me. Want my busted hairline I got because my cousin cuts my hair instead of a real barber? Take it. Want my bootleg Marbury shoes I got because I can't afford Jordans? Take them, too! Want my tired, dirty clothes I haven't had washed in a month, want the mother who can't wash them because her boyfriend took all the quarters? Want my brother's ten years up in county lock-up he got for banking the guy who banked our cousin? Take all that stuff.

What you told us today when school opened back up after the riots didn't make much sense, Miss K, because the first thing you said was, "I don't want to hear anything about what you all did the last few days." I get why you said that. You're a teacher, and you have to go tell when you know we did something illegal. You just want to protect us. But you also put these notebooks in our hands and told us to write in our journals. When we write in our journals, you always tell us to write what's on our minds. Well, you know that what's on all our minds since we last had school has everything to do with Freddy Gray, with burning things down, with running from the police, and with stealing everything that wasn't nailed down at Mondawmin Mall on Monday.

I was there, you know, at Mondawmin. I started over there right after school like most of us did, because everyone was saying we were going to march and take over the city from there. They were talking like we were Sherman's Army marching to burn down Atlanta. Yeah, I listen to some things you say. Everyone was talking righteous talk about a reckoning, and how our day had come. I'm telling you, we thought we were on our way to do a good thing. But the police were all over at Mondawmin. You couldn't get off the buses there. So folks tussled for a while, bricks and bottles, and I tried to see what was going on, but couldn't, and then someone said they'd broken into the mall, and if we couldn't clean up what was wrong with the city, at least we could clean up on everything in the Mondawmin Mall.

I admit, the first thing I thought of was getting some new kicks. My family acts like the decision for me to wear Marbury shoes is political, like we think it's criminal what a black superstar charges poor black families for shoes, but everyone can see through that. We don't even vote. So that big, white governor we got who just sent the National Guard here? Yeah, that's our bad, I guess.

Anyhow, I knew I wouldn't be able to get any shoes. The first place folks were headed was Foot Locker, and before I even got inside the mall, I saw all kinds of people running out with their hands full of shoe boxes.

Can you write this for me how I want it to sound, Miss Kovac?

Miss K, you're not going to believe me, but I went inside the mall and I didn't steal anything. I just watched. There wasn't anybody in there trying to stop anyone from stealing. People were fighting each other here and there over who got to steal what, but that was the only thing slowing anyone down. For the most part, as long as people weren't trying to make off with the same things, folks were actually helping each other out. I saw one guy put down his stack of stuff from GameStop long enough to help a girl who'd dropped what must have been about a thousand dollars' worth of hair. As long as you weren't competing for the same things, everyone there was all on the same team.

Would you believe someone was playing music? It wasn't the mall's music. They had turned that off. But people around here are creative, and somebody figured out how to put some Alicia Keys on while we robbed everything.

Okay, I've got to admit, even though I know you don't

want to hear it, that I did steal one thing. But I doubt they'll send any cops to arrest me for it. When I walked by the Cinnabon, I saw there were some rolls still behind the counter. They might have been there for a little while, but they looked pretty good to me.

You'll probably tell me that stealing something small is still stealing, but, like Kevin Hart says, "let me explain." I applied for a job at Cinnabon once, that same Cinnabon at Mondawmin. I needed to get some money for my brother's lawyer, and I figured I'd get to eat a lot if I worked there. I know you keep telling us that we have to stop eating all that processed sugar they sell to black people that gives us diabetes, but I love those damn things. I didn't get that job anyway, because the bus schedule didn't work from there to my house after they closed at night. I couldn't do anything for my brother, as a matter of fact.

I'm not saying all this right. You have to fix it for me. You know they don't have a Cinnabon in Sandtown-Winchester, where I'm from, where Freddy Gray was from. You think if they'd have had a Cinnabon where we live that Freddy would've had his head slammed around in a police van? No way. He'd have had his ass at the Cinnabon instead of doing whatever it was he did to get himself thrown in that van, and I'd have been there selling it to him.

Instead, Freddy is dead. They buried him, and then we all went to Mondawmin. I saw on the news how they were showing all the bad things Freddy did, saying he wasn't worth burning up a city for. But then that same news was making out that mom who slapped her kid around to be some kind of hero. If they had cameras in my neighborhood every day, they'd see moms beating up their sons like that pretty much all the time. She's no hero. I know that kid. If I had to bet on the one person I know most likely to go for a rough ride like Freddy Gray one day, it'd be him.

If she's a hero, then so is D'Andre's foster mom. She lets her boyfriend, who just got out of county lockup himself, beat D'Andre almost every day. D'Andre is easy to beat on. You've seen him. He has to wrap his belt around himself twice to keep his school uniform pants from falling down. He only stays in that home because his sister is there, too, and he doesn't want the boyfriend to get with his sister. Which is why he usually gets hit. So I guess his foster mom's boyfriend is also a hero, the social worker who doesn't notice what is going on is a hero and the judge who put him there is a hero. Mayor Blake is a hero and the cops are heroes. This town is full of damn heroes. Sounds like a nice place to live. But it isn't. You know it isn't, Miss K. I know you care about us, but I also know you wouldn't hang around here after school is over. You get back to your house in Howard County as soon as you can. And I don't blame you. Why would you want to eat a Cinnabon at Mondawmin when you can have a latte at Starbucks?

Will you tell this right for me? I ate that cinnamon roll while I sat in the food court. I was the only one sitting. Everyone was running and excited. For the first time, we could afford stuff we wanted at the store in our own neighborhood. The sun was coming in, Alicia Keys was singing, and suddenly I realized it was spring outside. I bet I felt like you feel on a Saturday morning in Howard County when you grade our papers while you're sitting outside at Starbucks. You must look around and see a wide open world and feel like you're free to do whatever you want in it.

Cinnabon used to be the place I failed to get my brother out of prison. This whole city is one big prison without a roof. But that roll was so sweet to eat there in the sunlight of the food court in the spring, for a minute it felt like I owned the place. We all felt like we owned something. For a minute, I remembered how you told me that Thurgood Marshall grew up where I grew up, and that seemed like something worth being proud of.

You've got to help me say this right for the people you know, the ones who see all this on the news.

When I finally had to leave, I walked home for miles through a burning city with icing all over my hands.

FROM THE PORCH

MARK SENKUS

early enough in the morning
sitting on the front porch
there is something of poetry in it
one fine splendor of aging
sitting in pajamas with dark roast
the cup heavy on the palms
in the still warming air
I hear children on the next street
laughing and playing as children
a new garage going up across the alley
making the slow sound of its construction
the neighbor college girl dashes out
to get something from her car parked curbside
in t-shirt and black underwear
a quite forgivable act when one is young
yellow and red brightness of shining tulips
peep through the wooden slats of fence
and of course there are the birds
always the birds
grackles and chickadees and starlings
pushing their territories against each other
retreating then pushing forward again
it is a lifelong process for them
and for us if we are lucky this lifetime
of gradual aging that bursts like a star

upon our laps
bringing us to sit on a porch on a bright
unfolding morning seeing and listening
to everything that we can
hoping for the children down the street
this steadily long life with its curious lengths
doled out from where it all started to here now
on this porch.

EVERYTHING NEATLY PUT AWAY

Kilby Allen

The smell of melting crayons, rich and kindergarteny, reminded Katy of her sister, Charlotte.

When they were little, Charlotte, wiser, the one who knew things, balanced crayons in the dips between electric radiator coils. They waited, and after two or three cartoons, the wax began to run down the sides, liquid color.

She remembered how Charlotte smeared it on her cheeks, two dark purple stripes, whiskers, war paint, how the wax crackled and itched as it dried.

That was a long time ago. Now Katy was alone and Charlotte, a memory. Or she was many memories all bound up in the walls, clothes left on hangers, secret smells shut away in a tin lunchbox.

Katy found her everywhere that summer, unexpectedly rushing headlong into forgotten moments, grief thickening the air here like gelatin. She couldn't wait to get out of the house.

After the funeral, she found the lunchbox in the back of Charlotte's closet. The tin *Fraggle Rock* lunchbox once held their crayons, but now inside were Charlotte's secret things: pictures, a journal from eighth grade, three neatly rolled joints, two condoms, notes written on ripped notebook paper, soft from rereading. Katy knew she shouldn't take the lunchbox with her, but couldn't imagine leaving it behind.

Tomorrow morning, she was leaving for camp. That summer

Katy was fifteen, as old as a person could be and still go to summer camp. Too old, probably, Katy thought. Last year she begged her mother not to iron the personalized lables— Property of: Katherine Graham—on every piece of clothing she owned.

Her mother did it anyway—at night—while everyone else was sleeping. She even ironed one on Katy's swimsuit.

This year her mother forgot.

Charlotte had been dead for ten months and twenty-two days. Katy knew because she crossed off each day in a little datebook, the size of a Gideon bible, that came free in the mail the week it all happened. On the cover, *Farm & Country Insurance* was printed under a glossy picture of an endless wheat field.

She understood that it was weird and wrong to mark off every day with a pink highlighter—like a countdown to prom, or something—but she couldn't seem to help herself. And when anyone mentioned the word, heaven, which seemed to happen too often lately, Katy now pictured infinite wheat fields under mostly clear skies.

She kept her calendar in the lunchbox with the rest of the things she didn't want her parents to find. Not that they were snoops, necessarily. Her mother used to be, but lately she'd lost interest, in that and just about everything else. But Katy needed these things. They were the real Charlotte, a Charlotte not even she knew.

Katy couldn't remember a time when the box was actually used for lunch. It had always been in Charlotte's room, full of magic markers and broken crayons. Now the Fraggles on the lid were rusted around the edges, and the family crayons were forgotten in a Folgers can with her mother's craft supplies. Katy doesn't remember when the box disappeared and was repurposed, but when she found it in the very back of Charlotte's closet, inside a cardboard box and buried beneath old sweatshirts, she felt the gut-punch of recognition and a fresh wash of loss.

What was inside made her feel something very different. Lined notebook paper folded into imperfect rectangles, fringe intact—these were Charlotte's love letters. Some were indecipherable, angular boy-scrawl, words like *LUV* and *4ever* floating to the surface. Most were from Isaac, Charlotte's high school boyfriend, but some were signed "M." A few weren't signed at all, and in different handwriting entirely, neater and rounder.

Katy couldn't glean much from these. They were mostly generic Valentine's Day stuff, studded with awkward, misappropriated movie lines. But a few phrases haunted her: *Meet me at the place,* and *remember the time in the graveyard?* and *I know how hard it must've been to tell me that.* These contained mysteries she could never solve.

Katy closed the lunchbox and put it behind her pillow in case her mother walked in. One by one she rolled her t-shirts into neat little tubes and stacked them in the trunk. Somewhere, in other parts of the house, her parents were avoiding each other. At least camp was loud, everyone always shouting and laughing and snoring.

Sometimes, walking through the house, it felt like she'd gone deaf. Then a stair would creak and everyone, shut away in their own rooms, nursing private grief, would collectively startle in the ruptured silence.

From far below the dryer buzzed, and Katy went downstairs for her laundry. In the kitchen her mother was wearing a bathrobe, sitting at the breakfast table, red eyes absently gazing at the television screen. She watched a cooking show about cakes. Someone was making realistic wildflowers out of fondant. On the table in front of her rested a paper plate heaped with spit-soaked pistachio shells.

"What time is Seth getting here in the morning?" her mother asked. It seemed to Katy that all her mother wanted to talk about these days was Seth, Katy's boyfriend. It was like she liked the idea of Katy having a boyfriend more than Katy did herself. "Look at that groom's cake. Dutch chocolate." Her mother put another pistachio in her mouth, sucking the salt. "Does Seth like chocolate?" she asked with her mouth full.

"We've been dating for three weeks, Mom." And besides, he lived down the street and spent most of his childhood in this very kitchen. She'd only reluctantly gone to junior prom with him and was surprised to find out that, in Seth's mind, it meant they were dating. It proved difficult to persuade him otherwise.

Katy thought of him as a human golden retriever: sweet, not so smart, but with big brown eyes that were impossible to disappoint. Also, he didn't treat her differently because she had a dead sister. He never talked about Charlotte, which was nice, even though Katy knew he missed her, too. Plus he was two years older and had a car, which seemed to impress her friends tremendously.

"I need to fold my laundry," Katy said, leaving her mother to chew in the green TV light.

"Don't stay up too late," her mother called after her, gaze never leaving the screen.

"I'm not." Tomorrow Seth would drive her to camp, two and a half hours alone together in a car. Honestly, Katy dreaded it. When Seth was her friend, *their* friend—Charlotte's and hers, it was easy to talk to him. They had fun.

Once, a few years ago, when Charlotte first got her license, the three of them drove to Jackson for the state fair. They ate funnel cakes and corndogs until Katy felt too queasy to ride any of the metal-shrieking, duct-taped midway rides. (At least that's what she told them.) So she waited in the wet straw below, watching them, bodies slung together on the tilt-a-whirl; the two of them upside down, clinging to each other in sweaty fear, strapped into the Gravitron.

After they rode all the rides, and Charlotte was ready to go home, it was Seth who insisted that they go to the 4-H livestock barn, which is all that Katy wanted to do the entire time they were at the fair. And when the cattle exhibit was closed when they got there, Seth was the one who helped her sneak in to pet the highland cow.

He gave her a boost so she could crane over the fence and touch its silken coat, more like a show dog's than a cow's, and the whole time her back was pressed against his chest. She could feel his heart beat, and in that moment, Katy loved Seth with the ferocity that only a twelve-year-old girl can manage.

But that was a long time ago, when she was still a kid. They both were, really, even though Seth was too tall even then, and he knew how to smoke cigarettes. Unlike the other boys, he never made fun of Katy.

Back then, though, he was Charlotte's golden retriever— only two years younger but so boyish. And that autumn Charlotte seemed, to Katy at least, suddenly and mysteriously grownup.

That was one of the last times the three of them spent an entire day together.

Things changed. Seth moved up to the high school with Charlotte, leaving Katy behind. Charlotte got a boyfriend, making Seth even more like a lovesick puppy.

Then things changed again. Just as Katy was catching up to them, Charlotte went to college and died.

And now Katy stood under the laundry room's bare bulb, folding hand-me-down sweatshirts with Charlotte's name fading from their iron-on tags. She unloaded the laundry piece by piece, folding on the washing machine lid. The laundry room was small and unfinished, just off the kitchen. It used to be a screened porch, so there was a door to the backyard.

Floorboards creaked out in the kitchen as her mother pushed away from the table and shuffled toward her. Katy didn't feel like talking.

"Goodnight, sweetheart," her mother said, peeking around the doorframe. Katy felt a wave of relief.

"Night, Mom," she said, towel pinched beneath her chin. As soon as her mother's footsteps faded away, Katy went back to folding and listened for the familiar muffled knock on the back door.

It would be Seth, sneaking over as soon as Katy's parents' light went out, just like he had since elementary school, when they used to creep into the cemetery at the end of the block, to scare themselves and play with Seth's glow-in-the-dark Frisbee. She missed the Frisbee nights.

Now there were other expectations. Mostly they sat under the World War One memorial angel and talked about the school newspaper. Seth was the assistant editor, and Katy covered Clubs. It gave them something to talk about that wasn't Charlotte.

Seth never wanted to talk about feelings, and that made the whole thing tolerable for her. She could pretend that they were still just pals, that he didn't sometimes look at her with different eyes, wanting something that she couldn't give him.

He was standing on the back steps, hugging himself against a chill, even though it was a warm night.

"Hey," she whispered through the screen door. He waited for a second, then opened the door himself and stepped lightly into the laundry room, avoiding the single creaky floorboard.

"Ready?" Seth showed her that he had a bottle of red wine, swiped from his mother's stockpile. He leaned in for a kiss, but Katy pretended not to notice and turned away, arms full of folded laundry.

"Let me get a sweatshirt," she said and tiptoed up the stairs, leaving him to stand there in the bare-bulb light.

Upstairs, Katy had to walk past Charlotte's closed door to

get to her room. She hadn't been in there in a long time.

Charlotte lived in a dorm room, hundreds of miles away, when she died. The layers of her childhood had been dismantled and disrupted, so even before it happened, Katie could already feel her absence in the room. There were still faded Book Fair animal posters taped inside the closet door, but most of Charlotte's clothes were still packed up in anonymous moving boxes. No one could open them, so they remained in the middle of the room where their father stacked them.

Katy found herself standing in front of Charlotte's closed door when she made the sudden decision. Tonight she would have sex with Seth. As soon as the idea came into her head, she knew that it was true. Katy took a condom from Charlotte's lunchbox, turned it over in her hands, checked the expiration date (good for another four months).

Did Charlotte buy this? A whole box? What happened to the others? Katy tried to imagine Charlotte's lovers. What did they look like?

Katy slid one of Charlotte's joints and the condom into the back pocket of her jeans. She didn't want to risk waking her parents by running water, but she put on a clean pair of underwear and crept downstairs.

Seth was sitting at the kitchen table in the dark.

They stepped out into the May night. The dark vibrated with the songs of crickets and frogs from the ditches around the cemetery. Under the angel Seth seemed nervous and tried to hold her hand, but it was awkward.

He took both her hands in his, then dropped one, but his grip was too tight. He swung his arm when they walked. It was all wrong. Finally Katy squeezed his hand and let it drop. She put her hands in her hoodie pocket, safely out of reach.

She was wearing one of Charlotte's zip-up sweatshirts, red, and too warm, but it felt like a cape, a security blanket.

Seth spoke in stock dialogue. Katy was reminded of the love letters. He was saying what he was supposed to say. Half of the time she felt like he was delivering remembered lines from a movie. That was how he talked with his friends, in sketch comedy routines and film scenes.

"You're so beautiful," Seth said, "it hurts to look at you." He tried to brush her hair out of her face, but his fingers caught in a snaggle.

"Ouch." Katy pulled away and put her hair up in a quick ponytail.

"Sorry." It all reminded her how hard he was trying, and how she just couldn't muster the feelings she knew she was supposed to have. They sat in silence for a little while. The grass beneath them was dry and scratchy. She couldn't remember the last time it rained.

Katy wondered if she would be broken forever. Did she feel anything like this before Charlotte died? She never had a boyfriend before, and only kissed two guys before Seth, both at summer camp.

Katy put her arm around him. She could try too.

"Want some," Seth asked, pouring warm, cheap wine into coffee mugs. He handed her one. It read *You are Beary Special* and was covered in hearts and teddy bears. Katy took a deep swallow. It tasted like Kool-Aid and battery acid.

"I have this." Katie showed him the joint.

"Cross country," Seth said, waving it away.

"It's summer. Months until your pee test," she said, and lit it with a kitchen match. It was old and dry, and the smoke tasted like burning dust. She passed it to Seth, and he took a long drag, just like she knew he would. He would do pretty much anything she asked him.

He seemed to genuinely feel something like love for her. He was able to do that, and it made her jealous somehow, and frightened.

When he picked her up for prom, she could tell something

was different. He wasn't the boy who followed Charlotte anymore. That night he kissed her and it felt like he meant it.

It all made her feel like she was in a play and somehow she never had the right script, and the costumes didn't fit.

Last week he took her to the graduation after-party. She was one of the only freshmen, or former freshmen, but no one seemed to care. The party lasted all night long. It was a campout on someone's farmland. Katy went to pee in the woods and heard rustling animal noises close by.

One of the tents was lurching, lurching, pitching. And then she realized what was happening. Later she found out it was Shelly Cooper and Rodney Richards going at it, performatively, she thought, their tent just barely outside the campfire glow.

She had never been so close to people having actual sex before. She couldn't believe that anyone could just have sex anywhere, right in front of her, even, separated from the world by only a thin sheet of green nylon. They sounded like creatures, not people, in something close to pain.

Katy moved away, stepping on a stick that broke, gunshot loud, but Shelley and Rodney didn't seem to notice. She went to find Seth and brought him to the tent.

He was very drunk, but he didn't laugh. Katy kept saying that she *couldn't believe they would just do it there, how gross*. But Seth didn't say anything. She didn't understand what he was thinking, but it scared her. She jokingly suggested that they just go do it in the woods, too, but he said no. Katy was surprised by a sudden stab of hurt, but mostly felt relieved.

Since then, she imagined that Seth had been thinking about the campout, too. The wine and weed made her feel like the ground underneath them was a softly rolling wave. She kissed him, unbuttoned his pants. She couldn't imagine putting his penis in her mouth, she just wanted to have sex and get it over with.

"Want to?" she asked.

"Can I take off your shirt?" he asked. She pulled it over her head before he could reach her. Up to that point, the most they'd done together were a couple of hand jobs and clothed heavy petting. They were both high and giggly.

She didn't get wet, really, but ripped open the condom wrapper with her teeth and tried to roll it onto him, but Seth took over. Then he couldn't get it in. It wouldn't fit.

"Can you help?" he whispered, but it hurt so much she couldn't really tell where anything was down there, which parts went where. It was all just pain, sharp when she breathed and then dull and insistent all the time.

She tried to relax, tried to imagine that her vagina was enormous, like she read in a book once, but it didn't work. Finally, after an endless two minutes, the dullness had been taken over by the sharpness, and she could almost imagine why it might be fun if it didn't hurt so much, but suddenly it was over, and he was sweating, clinging to her.

In that instant she just wanted him off, away from her. His weight and smell and vulnerability were repulsive.

Seth gathered himself and rolled off, pulling on his pants almost immediately. Katy felt ashamed and very naked, ashamed that part of her wanted him to hold her, wanted to be held like a weak thing, told that she was okay. In that moment she hated herself.

"Did you ever come here with Charlotte," Katy asked. She knew it was the wrong thing to say at the worst time. Seth looked suddenly stricken, and walked over to the bushes to puke spectacularly.

"It must be the pot. Not you," he said when he came back, wiping his mouth on his shirttail. He picked up his wine mug, took a sip, swished, and spat.

Katy pulled on her sweatshirt, then looked down to see a thin line of blood, trickling down her leg. She used one of her socks to mop between her legs, and it come back black in the moonlight. She threw the soiled sock under a bush and lined her panties with the other, then carefully pulled on her jeans.

You are okay. You are fine, she told herself.

Seth gathered up their mugs, the bottle, and then ground the roach into the dirt.

"Where did you put the thing," she asked, meaning the condom.

"In the bushes. I wouldn't go over there if I were you," he said. But she walked over, smelled vomit, and saw the sad little blue condom, lying in the grass. She kicked leaves over it, and felt horribly alone.

Seth insisted on walking her back to her house, but she wanted to get as far away from him as possible and could tell that he felt the same way. And tomorrow morning, he would be there to drive her to camp, something they both now dreaded, though they would never admit it.

On the back steps they awkwardly hugged goodnight. Katy could feel blood seeping through her jeans as she walked upstairs.

Upstairs she rinsed her jeans in the bathroom sink—the bathroom she used to share with Charlotte. She put in a tampon to stop the bleeding, but twenty minutes later her underwear was soaked through. She took out the tampon and it was totally dry, clean and white.

In the back of the under sink cabinets she found a dusty, industrial-sized box of overnight maxi-pads left from before she was old enough for tampons. The pad was giant, bigger than her cotton underwear, so the edges poked out. Even with pajamas covering it, she could still hear the rustling.

Katy finished packing, placed Charlotte's lunchbox in her trunk under a stack of t-shirts. She should be asleep. Seth would be there to pick her up in six hours.

She walked back down the darkened hall for a glass of water. Her father was asleep, snoring, behind his office door, listening to an audiobook. For the last several months he'd been playing all the *Chronicles of Narnia* books over and over. He read them to Katy and Charlotte when they were little.

This was the first summer that Charlotte wouldn't be at camp. Katy had never been there alone.

Last summer Charlotte was around too much. Katy totally avoided the boat dock, where her sister was a lifeguard and waterfront counselor. She wished then that Charlotte would just go away, that everyone would stop referring to her as Charlotte's little sister.

On her way back to her room, Katy stopped in front of her sister's door. She turned the knob and a puff of stale air escaped into the hall. Inside, the boxes were still stacked, dust had gathered on the horseshow ribbons above her desk. The quilt on the bed was old—a great grandmother made it—but when Katy threw herself facedown onto the bed, it didn't smell like Charlotte anymore.

She lay on Charlotte's bed, nose pressed into the pillows, searching for any remaining Charlotte-ness. Under one of the pillows she found a patchy stuffed rabbit—Pete.

She wondered how long he had been there, exiled when Charlotte when away to college. He'd gone everywhere with her before that, Katy remembered, sleepovers, their aunt's house in Nashville, camp. She wondered how he must feel now.

Katy pulled back the quilt and snuggled under the scentless sheets. With Pete squeezed into the crook of her arm, she closed her eyes. The clock on the bedside table read 3:44, but who knew if it was changed for daylight savings.

Underneath her pajama pants, the maxi-pad felt like a diaper. She knew she was supposed to feel different now, grown up.

But in the morning when she woke, her mother standing over, she knew that she was the same. Everything was the same. Though at least now, she understood that from now on, she traveled alone.

YET ANOTHER BIRTHDAY

Bibhu Padhi

I know someone is dying
this moment into me,
choosing to give away
to this body his unknown, unpredicted
slices of life, as if
each moment was a further life.

Generous breaths pause
on each cell on this body,
as if they looked for
a habitat that they would find
their very own, something
that was long overdue.

I wonder if this body deserves
the gifts that arrive every moment,
without its asking, from places
that might have hardly known
what it needs, affectionate extensions.

Today I know how bodies, distanced
by unseen hands, are indeed together,
at one place, through all time,   defying
differences that fate
so skilfully invents but doesn't know
their private wishes that float on
to all time, one place.

I am here and know how friendships
about to close, are quietly renewed.

A SPOT OF BODY, WITHOUT BLOOD

Bibhu Padhi

A body lies on a road in the north,
under fog and winter.
A hazy picture of mice
scampering away onto the road
from under its thin sheet of
helplessness, is all there is,
except a sheer white night
that seems to tease the warmth
of our homes, our extended lives.

Talks of help and national loss
continue all through day
and night, loud and clear, on
handsome faces, against a music
that is meant to be sad and near.
What is the purpose
of this show of love on a day
that has darkened earlier than usual?
Did the body ever know
what it was, why it was here,
what happened to it on the night
when it was worshipping
the difficult, freezing cold?

I don't know what I can do
from here, but all I know is
there is a body lying somewhere
in a city in the north, now hunted
and disturbed by creatures
we hate to be with, at the end of
a long struggle with himself
and a whimsical, fantastic god.

THE ORCHESTRATED WILD

Douglas S. Jones

The piano follows everywhere I go. Everywhere I go I am
followed by keys and pedals, by the possibility of chords and
    scales.

In my shadow the baby grand opens like an oyster. It is brimming
    with pearls.
It's not my piano. It's not mine to play. Its sounds come to me like
    hyenas,

their brindle muzzles shining with kill. But it's more than in my
    shadow. In darkness—the real
kind, the true kind, the kind that blocks out light and breath and clocks,
    the kind we know

but never speak of or even try to understand, the piano is there.
    Part string, part percussion. Part
pearl. All tooth. Part death, but not dead.   I'm telling you this
    because I hope

you will tell me what orchestra is trailing behind you, just out of
    sight. What tuba is waiting
to be breathed into a moan, what oboe or flute or tympano stalks
    you like you are an animal,

what instrument waits silent as the conductor's scavenger
    coattails, silent
as the baton itself hanging just above the breast, waiting for all
    the sound in the world to drop

like a tooth into the marrow, like a pearl into its dark glass of
    wine.

NO BIRDS SINGING IN THE FIELD

Sophie Wolfram

People often confuse the Mississippi Delta with the Mississippi River Delta, which is where the Mississippi River dumps all it has collected from the millions of acres it drains into the Gulf of Mexico. Every year until European settlers began building levees along the Lower Mississippi, some of that water used to spill out of the river and flood millions of acres of the boggy, low-lying land a few hundred miles north of the Gulf. When we talk about the Mississippi Delta known for cotton, the blues, Emmett Till, and Medgar Evers, it is to that oft-flooded region that we refer. The Mississippi Delta is neither a true river delta nor triangular in shape, yet the name has stuck. Memphis sits about twenty-five miles above its northern boundary, and Vicksburg marks its southern tip. Driving east from the river, the Mississippi Delta ends when you climb your first hill. The weather report on the radio station that wakes me up at five each morning calls it the ArkLaMiss Delta. But in the Delta, everyone just calls it the Delta.

Even an hour before sunrise, the morning is hot. Uncomfortable in ill-fitting professional clothes, I trundle half-awake into the Delta State University dining hall for coffee, toast, and cottage cheese. The mosquitoes are so thick in the air that picking them out of my food becomes part of the morning routine. At the school bus loading zone, other summer school staff members have already sweat through their button-down shirts. They pile into decades-old yellow buses for the hour-long drives across the Delta's endless corn and soy fields to their posts in Indianola, Itta Bena, Tutwiler, Clarksdale, Webb, and Sumner. There they pass mornings in sessions on diversity and inclusion, planning and execution, and classroom management; afternoons are spent playing teacher to students in summer school for credit recovery.

It is the summer of 2010, and I am one of hundreds of new teachers spending a sultry six weeks at DSU in Cleveland, Mississippi, where Teach For America holds its training for many of the corps members who will go on to placement sites in rural areas all over the country. I will stay in the Delta, but, like most corps members, I don't know yet where I'll teach or even what grade I'll teach. My assignment is simply "Mississippi Delta, Secondary Math." Each morning, the bus that ferries my summer school cohort to our summer school site in Tallahatchie County leaves at 5:43 a.m., and it waits for no one. Most nights, we plan lessons and pore over training material until around midnight. During the three-hour post-teaching afternoon sessions, many of us remain standing in order to keep from falling asleep.

I am developing a tunnel vision that allows me to maximize my efficiency as I race through each day. I am also learning to expand my "locus of control," which is the language TFA uses to describe all of the student behaviors and mindsets teachers can influence. The idea is that teachers who perceive their locus of control as very narrow will be quicker to throw up their hands in the face of challenging circumstances, whereas teachers who believe their locus of control is much larger will find creative solutions to thorny issues that arise in their classrooms. There will always be a world outside of school, and we cannot control what happens in our students' lives out there. We must compensate by maximizing the influence we have when class is in session and the students are in front of us. While I cannot make a dent in poverty, racism, and crumbling rural infrastructure, I can fine-tune assessment questions, craft catchy lesson hooks, and sharpen the key points of geometry lessons. The message I am absorbing is that my vision should be directed inward toward my own mindsets and practices.

1.

My placement school is Park Elementary, in Greenwood, Mississippi, an hour east of Cleveland. I teach seventh grade math. I am diligent in my planning and serious about classroom management. I cling to my tunnel vision like a life preserver in a sea of frustrating scheduling decisions, academic unpreparedness, lack of curricular resources, and the constant sound of paddles striking children's backsides. Many days one student or another, breathless either from running all the way down the hall or from the thrill of having an important job to do, interrupts my planning period to declare, "Ms. Wolfram! Mr. Brown needs a witness!" I walk down the hall as the messenger skips back to class and subtly avert my eyes as the wooden board smacks the unlucky offender one, two, or three times, depending on the severity of the offense. Duty done, I return to my classroom to take a few bites of lunch and prepare for sixth period.

As my first school year winds down (a process that begins in mid-April but accelerates after state tests in May) the number of "Fun Fridays" increases in turn. Fun Friday, basically a three-hour recess, is usually announced a day or two in advance and is used to bribe students to stay out of trouble through the latter half of the week. Otherwise, they are doomed to fill out worksheets in Ms. McLeod's room all afternoon while everyone else gets to play outside.

On Fun Fridays the kids can purchase snacks from a table in the cafeteria. Where the proceeds go remains a mystery to me, but as with most secrets in Delta schools, the rumors are probably less colorful than the truth. Their options include pickled eggs; hot chips (spicy Doritos); hot chips with cheese (open a bag of spicy Doritos, fill a ladle with nacho cheese, and pour into the open bag); Kool-Aid pickles (what they sound like); and an assortment of flavors of Airheads.

A tangle of dress-code-abiding blue, red, and white polo shirts and knee-length khaki shorts crowds around the snack table, looping sometimes three or four times until we sell out and someone puts the money away who-knows-where. Then they explode outside with the short-lived sugar-and-chemical-based vitality that comes from candy and the highly addictive crackle and burn of hot chips.

The school grounds include a blacktop ringed with basketball hoops in various stages of decay and a vast, featureless field. No playground equipment. Generous trees along the edge of the field provide some shade, which the older girls take advantage of to keep the sun from darkening their skin. The bigger boys play basketball. The 4th and 5th graders, along with some of the younger-at-heart older kids, dance with abandon to "Get Low," "Bedrock" ("Call me Mr. Flinstone, I can make your bed rock"), and "Sexy and I Know It" ("I got passion in my pants and I ain't afraid to show it, show it, show it, show it.")

2.

I run almost every day. I know it is wearing on my knees, but it keeps feelings of worthlessness at bay after days of "Shut up talkin' to me" and "Get outta my face," favorite refrains of my seventh grade girls. Entering my bedroom when I get home, I change into running clothes before my brain has time to catch up to my tricks and stop me. By the time I'm asking myself, "Don't you want to *nap*?" I am out the door. Small angry dogs nip at my heels until the hairpin turn near the end of the street.

Today is a Sunday early in the spring of my second year, and

I am in high spirits because not only has nobody verbally abused me today, but also I am going to fly home to New York this afternoon for a week-long break. Driving on I-55 north out of the Delta and up to the airport in Memphis always feels like breaking the fourth wall: freeing, revealing, a little shocking, a reminder that I hover on the threshold in this place, both audience and actor. There is a lightness in the air today, and running feels effortless. A little experience in the classroom has allowed me to shed my tunnel vision, and I have started taking time now and then to pay attention to this place outside the narrow set of immediately obvious factors that shape my students' lives. Spring is my favorite thing about the Delta. Magnolia blossoms as large as dinner plates cloak whole neighborhoods in their fragrance, evoking, it seems to me, the spirit of another era.

My standard route takes me from my house on Taylor Drive in North Greenwood across the Yalobusha River and left on a gravel road that skirts the first cornfield north of town. Last season's stubble still stands here, solitary. I hear no birds singing, no rustling in the brush on the other side of the road. A dog carcass that I peer at despite myself each time I pass continues its slow, anonymous decay in the ditch.

For me, running in this place is peaceful because it seems absolutely separate from the world in which I am failing to reach children who need help. The temperature is perfect today, and I am so energized by the thought of going home that I decide to do a full ten miles. I trace the edge of the field and head north on Money Road and turn around when I reach the Tallahatchie River. On my way back I cut through the corn field on a narrow path between rows of rotting stalks. Plentiful moisture early in the season has yielded a mud that is thick and sloppy. It doesn't splash; it slides and pulls and only reluctantly belches up my shoes with my feet still in them step after straining step. My quads and hamstrings delight in the tug-of-war, and I feel free in the solitude of a Delta early spring morning.

3.

In December of 2010, my first year, Leflore County Sheriff Ricky Banks is speaking up about a young black man who was recently found hanging from an oak tree in North Greenwood, in a field very much in the white part of town, along my running route. Frederick Jermaine Carter, Banks says, "had a mental condition and a history of wandering off." His family argues that his mental health was just fine and is requesting that a second autopsy be performed outside the state of Mississippi. The attorney representing Mr. Carter's family decries the county's failure to follow procedure: "A crime scene was never established. They never roped the scene off and this has not been treated as a crime. There is no reason to believe that he would commit suicide." The idea of a black man hanged from a tree in the Mississippi Delta evokes in my imagination another era of American history, but like the rich perfume of magnolias, the hatred and fear surrounding moments like these still hangs heavy, though unspoken, in the heart of the rural South.

The only reference ever made to it at school is a full year later when my student Tyanna warns her classmates, "Don't go over to North Greenwood. Them folks'll kill you." Even then, I wonder which act of violence she is referring to. In the Delta it sometimes feels as though history, like the landscape itself, is flat. Events one hundred and fifty years ago press up next to what you ate for lunch yesterday. Tyanna would never say whether she was referring to Mr. Carter or to other lynching victims from farther back in history, nor would she necessarily have a specific reference point in mind. More likely she is drawing from a thick haze of unspoken collective memory too painful to address directly but too significant to ignore.

4.

I live at 534 Taylor Drive, and Wes lives one house to the left, at 532. Wes sides with the strays of the community, and from what I can tell he is a bit of a stray himself. He grew up thirty-some years ago in a trailer in the unincorporated community of Sidon about ten miles south of Greenwood. Sidon is now 95 percent black and is where many of my students live; I wonder if the demographic shift accounts for Wes's migration to this side of town. A fellow teacher at Park, herself born and raised in Sidon, informed me once that Sidon is the incest capital of Mississippi. Unofficially, I assume.

Wes points out spots on his torso and shoulders where he's been stabbed and shot at, and he boasts about his former career flipping cars. I don't know what "flipping cars" means, but I get the sense that it's illegal and that he might think I'm naïve for asking, so I pretend to understand. In high school, Wes dated my across-the-street neighbor Kim, but he's married now, and he doesn't get into much trouble anymore. He's a machinist, so he makes good money fixing farm equipment on contract. When he's not working, he volunteers at the pound. His yard is full of dogs no one else would adopt, and they greet me with kisses and muddy paws when I come home from work. When the police came recently to round up strays, he threatened them with a lead pipe, he tells me. I can tell that he's proud of that.

One late-spring evening we are standing where grass meets asphalt at the edge of my front yard. The back door of my hatchback is open before us, and the car is stuffed with crates of pots and pans and silverware, duffel bags, and boxes of books. I've completed my two-year teaching commitment in Leflore County, and I recently accepted a job teaching at a charter school in New York City. Wes and I have been talking about what it will be like to live in New York and what I'll miss about Greenwood. He tells me about a niece of his living in

New York and gives me her name in case I run into her there. As we talk, he helps me arrange and rearrange the contents of my life in the back of my car until we can close the door

The next day he loads my mattress and box spring into his pickup and gives me a lift to a friend's house on River Road, where I'll stack them against a wall in a spare bedroom until I find someone who wants to buy them. As we bump down the road, he gets to telling me about his family history for the first time. I listen politely but somewhat absent-mindedly until I hear him say, "My uncle's name is Byron de la Beckwith. They said he shot that man, Medgar Evers, in Jackson in '63, but see he couldn't've done it. He was in Greenwood the whole time, see." He says all this casually, as if it should be no surprise to me. I've thought plenty before about how my students' grandparents and great-grandparents were sharecroppers and civil rights activists, so why wouldn't my neighbors' parents and grandparents have been landowners and klansmen? "Whole bunch o' folks sayin' he was in Greenwood. How'd he shoot him all the way in Jackson, then?" Then, "This house right here? Lemme help you get them up the stairs."

5.

Fifteen hundred years ago bottomland hardwood forests dominated the Mississippi Delta. Bald cypresses rose from the mire, their knobby knees poking out above the surface of the water to stabilize their enormous trunks. These forests still dot the landscape, haunting reminders of how thoroughly exploitative agricultural practices have transformed the nature of both the place and its imported people. Beginning several decades before the Civil War, white settlers and droves of slaves they brought with them began clearing the forests, establishing vast fields for the cultivation of cotton. For the next hundred and sixty years cotton was king in the Delta, and the bottomlands and hardwood forests suffered the consequences; 70 percent of the original wetlands in the Delta have been lost.

The October sun slants in the car window golden and shimmering in the late afternoon. It's a Friday, and I decided this afternoon to explore what lies north of my running route on Money Road. A hand-painted sign riddled with buckshot points me right to Six Mile Lake, and I swerve hard to join the rutted road to the lake.

A call from my sister in California to tell me that she is pregnant and expecting a baby due in May offers a welcome reminder that I am a visitor here; I can have a bad day at school, but the most important parts of my life are elsewhere. Periodic reminders like these help me recover from long days and long weeks. My outsider status seems both to protect me from experiencing the full weight of the tragedy and injustice constantly on display here and to distance me so that, spared the trauma, I can never quite seem to understand the place.

I hang up and pull back onto the road past tucked-away houses where, I imagine, the kinds of people who hunt and fish in this state must live. The lake is not accessible from the road; all of it is adjacent to private property, and "No Trespassing" signs stand guard next to each of the cabins on stilts overlooking the lake. It is a beautiful afternoon, and I will not be deterred. I find the property where it seems least likely that anyone is home and edge toward the shoreline. The sun has sunken lower now and glows orange over the water, which reflects back the shadows of the tupelo and cypress that rise out of the thick brown mud like weary witnesses of human folly through the ages. Six Mile Lake is part of the McIntyre Scatters, a wetland area popular among duck hunters. The Yalobusha River snakes through scattered oxbow lakes and bayous, wetlands undergirded by a foundation of mud.

It is mud like this mud that a Navy detachment of 100 sailors dredged in 1964 when they searched for James Chaney, a black civil rights worker from Mississippi, and Andrew Goodman and Michael Schwerner, white activists from New

York. The three were participating in Freedom Summer, a massive initiative to register voters, build community centers, and teach in 'freedom schools.' They went missing on June 23, 1964. FBI agents arrived to begin searching the same day. Investigators found the charred wreckage of the station wagon belonging to the three men in Bogue Chitto swamp, 125 miles southeast of Six Mile Lake. The events fixed the nation's gaze on racism in Mississippi, as *The New York Times* published articles with headlines such as "Mississippi: A Profile of the Nation's Most Segregated State."

But none of this was new or surprising, I imagine, to the trees, turtles, and birds of Mississippi's forests and swamps. Between 1887 and 1950, 579 people were lynched in Mississippi, 18 of those in Leflore County. Most black residents of the Delta were sharecroppers and tenant farmers in this era, and the number of lynchings was historically highest during the time of year when accounts were being settled and in years when the region's economy was weak. Before finding Chaney, Goodman, and Schwerner, Navy sailors pulled eight black bodies out from the muddy waters of Mississippi's rivers and few remaining acres of flooded forest.

I think about calling my mom to tell her how beautiful the lake is. I am so accustomed to corn and soy that I can hardly believe such beauty exists here in Leflore County. Something about the place feels like it belongs here. It doesn't feel lonely like the fields north of town. I imagine that I am partaking in an experience of place that is somehow more authentic than what my students have access to. I wish they had more access to nature; naively I wonder if they might find the connection and acceptance here that it often seems they are missing.

7.

There is a black sign with gold lettering alongside Money Road ten miles north of Greenwood that is easy to miss. It stands next to a crumbling two-story red-brick structure with a sign on the boarded up front door that reads "PRIVATE PROPERTY: Violators Will Be Prosecuted." Two-by-fours on the second story jut forward at uncomfortable angles like broken bones that have pierced through skin. Some sort of climbing vine I am not familiar with is slowly devouring the decrepit facade. Its leaves are changing color and show a deep crimson in the warm sun. A photo posted online and dated 2009 shows a brick wall behind the wooden skeleton on the second story, but by October of 2011 that wall has crumbled. I wonder in how many more years this relic of a building will be dust. The historical marker reads, "BRYANT'S GROCERY: Fourteen-year-old Emmett Till came to this site to buy candy in August 1955. White shopkeeper Carolyn Bryant accused the black youth of flirting with her, and shortly thereafter, Till was abducted by Bryant's husband and his half brother. Till's tortured body was later found in the Tallahatchie River." The plaque was dedicated on May 18, 2011. Before that, the store stood vacant like any of the other vacant storefronts on the block.

The murderers were tried in Sumner, Mississippi and acquitted by a jury of twelve white neighbors of the defendants after deliberations lasting a mere sixty-five minutes. The next year, J.W. Milam and Rob Bryant, the murderers, sold the story of the murder to *Look* magazine for $4,000. Shortly after the incident, Bryant's Grocery was boarded up. The man who currently owns the property, Harry Tribble, is the son of one of the jurors who acquitted Milam and Bryant.

It is quiet in Money. Fewer than 100 people live here, and trains pass through only rarely. It is at once sinister and harmless, victim and torturer, ugly and beautiful. So when friends and family ask, "What's it like in Mississippi?" I don't know what to say. I think I know what they want to hear. Something simple. Maybe they want to feel that they understand what keeps the

South stuck in the mire of racism and poverty. Maybe they want to be reassured that they are above such baseness and struggle. Maybe they want to believe that I, a reasonably intelligent, clear-eyed northerner, might be able see the root of the problems here. But to me it seems more complicated than that. I know that there is something here I cannot understand. The stillness of the spot where I stand belies the frenzied, layered complexity of its history. No moment here can be just one thing, and no person who is not from here can ever feel it all at once.

8.

Donquez and Tyrah are engaged in conversation. We are in the midst of dismissal, and the students in my seventh period class are waiting for their buses to be called. Donquez and Tyrah both ride bus 49, which is always among the last to leave. I am standing where I am supposed to be, in the doorway of the classroom, so that I can monitor my own students and students in the hall, who are supposed to walk, not run, for their buses. For the first twenty minutes or so of dismissal, which somehow regularly runs for about forty minutes, I require my students to read. I have assembled a classroom library of donated books. I can see that many of the kids, despite grumbling early in the year, are absorbed. Most students have left at this point, and I let the remaining few talk while they wait.

Donquez is one of my favorite students. On the first day of school I called out "DonKez?" while taking attendance, and among giggles from his classmates he shot me a steely look as he corrected, "It's Don-KWEZ." His lanky, bird-like frame hauls around enormous basketball shoes that are his pride and joy, and he idolizes LeBron James. When he does his work, his handwriting is one-of-a-kind. It loops gracefully and strangely with idiosyncratic flourishes, but most days he keeps his head on his desk and refuses to write. Like many of the boys I teach, though, his craving for approval lurks close to the surface, and it shines through when he finds out he got a tricky problem right or gets a sticker for a day of participating in class. Donquez lost both of his parents under circumstances I don't completely understand, but I have heard it might have been cancer. He lives with his grandmother and his sister, who is in the eighth grade and just had a baby. He is very hard to reach.

I knew about Tyrah before she met me, because her teachers from last year warned me about a quiet girl who stabbed a classmate in the face with a ballpoint pen repeatedly until a teacher pulled her off the boy. The boy she attacked had made a mean joke about Tyrah's little sister, Joelle, and that set her off. Tyrah spent two weeks in the alternative school, where it is rumored the walls are padded, before returning to Park Elementary. Her teachers let me know that she lives with her grandmother and her little sister; her parents died in a murder-suicide a few years ago. She and Donquez aren't in the same social circle, but they know each other from the therapy group Ms. Sias, the social worker, runs after school once a week. Once I tried to refer an unhappy student to Ms. Sias, and she told me, "I'd love to take her, but I really only have room in my caseload for the kids who are most likely to shoot up the school."

Tyrah is a Class A nerd, and we get along well. She struggles in math but loves to read, and other seventh graders rarely deign to be seen with her. So it surprises me to see Donquez deeply engrossed in conversation with her. I watch from the back of the room; after-school noise in the hallway makes it impossible for me to hear what they're saying. Their bodies are turned toward each other. Tyrah rests her head in her hand and one elbow on her desk. Donquez points his knees straight into the aisle between the desks and leans forward to listen, cupping his chin in both hands. Tyrah is speaking, and I can see in

Donquez's eyes and in his posture that he is wholly engaged. He cocks his head this way and that, nodding slowly on occasion. The conversation might last thirty seconds, maybe five minutes, but the depth of the connection between them is unmistakable. This moment of such unguarded openness between them seems to cast into relief all that is warped and crumbling and ugly around them, making it visible for the fleeting moments while the conversation lasts.

9.

Sarah arrived at school in October. She is one of four white kids in her grade. The white students are usually among the worst off, because if their families had the choice they would be at the private school, Pillow Academy, or at least at a Greenwood City school; they don't come to the county schools unless things are pretty dire. She told Ms. Howell, the secretary, that her daddy couldn't afford to get her and her siblings uniforms so that's why they're just starting school this month. Sarah can't read and lacks basic number sense. Her brow furrows with frustration and bewilderment when I introduce her to the idea of adding one and another number on her fingers. She always wears a ribbon in her hair, and her one white polo shirt shows the dirt that accumulates between laundry cycles. The teacher next door told me that last week she had sex with Sammie Steward in the bathroom. She doesn't have the social awareness to keep her mouth shut about her father's virulent racism. Sarah is a sad story, but she is not a sweet girl. She recently moved to a new home because her old one burned down. Her old home was a few houses down the street from where a friend of mine lives; it is rumored on the block to have been a crack house, but there is no way to know.

There is something that they all share, my stray-dog neighbor and his murderous uncle; Medgar Evers, Emmett Till, and Frederick Jermaine Carter; Donquez and Tyrah and Sarah and those sugar-addled fourth graders dancing on the field; the cotton that replaced the trees, and the corn and soy that replaced the cotton; and the silent bald cypresses that have watched it all. Just beyond my grasp, it is a quality I never succeed in putting my finger on. It is a quality rooted in a place where deep history lurks just under the surface, where nature and culture are subtly, troublingly, and inextricably bound. These people and places are knit together and layered and held in place by generations of family history, by reverberating violence, by lack of resources, sometimes by an inability to thrive anywhere else. Good and evil, past and present, victim and victimized, they are all rooted in the same thick Mississippi mud.

WOVEN WATER

John L. Stanizzi

after "Woven Water" (mixed media) by Barbara Hocker

She sang beyond the genius of the sea.
The Idea of Order at Key West
—Wallace Stevens

More than once we hear him address the sea;
the *rage for order*, as Stevens says, is *blessed,*
and even our dreams, as they wind across the width
of the ocean, soundlessly, have taken shape,
have reconstructed the day to resemble the sea,
the quiet boats, the night which has suffused
the spaces between the lights with zones of dark,
the rolling dusk, the shards of living shadow
absorbing the night, enchanting the careless passage
through which we tumble, portal of ghostly stars
where that which we have captured we must grasp
and hold it up against what has become
an idea engendered by the pen we hold,
a simple weaving of what we have imagined
with what we take for truth. We bring them both
together in our way, and seal them there
within the illusion that we have created order.

And when the demarcations of our musings
begin to feel *like a single thing* we are
inspired to deconstruct and make again
that thought which we, at first, could not call ours,
that empty, breathless chaos we'll try to arrange
against the water that wears away the stones.

GLOAMING

PHIL HEARN

I wake up and the drapes are lined with sun. I don't hear Mary in the kitchen, but she's not next to me either. Not that she'd fit anyway—my bed's half the size it was yesterday. Did she say something about ordering a new one? I thought I told her not to be so loose with the checkbook.

I don't know if it's mine or Mary's, but I brush my teeth with the only one on the counter. My arms actually ache while I'm doing it. They've turned to twigs since the plant closed. And Harper said early retirement would be a good thing. *Every day is yours, Rick. Use your savings, travel to the pyramids or some shit. Meet a mummy.*

The calendar says June 1st. I cross it off with a pencil now because I know I'll forget in the evening. The picture above the days shows a young couple walking arm-in-arm on a beach. Why do I have to look at these strangers for a whole month? Mary always buys the corniest one, flips through it in the bookstore and flashes the different months at me, *Isn't this Easter bunny just precious?* Sometimes she mistakes me for the damn kid.

I hope Drew didn't miss the bus again. Ms. Bullock said he'd fail out if he skipped one more time. Course, it's his own fault if he does. *Go ahead and drop out, buddy—the world needs janitors too.*

On my way to the kitchen I lift the urn off the mantle and

wrap my arms around it. Mary, my Mary. I pray to God that you're still somewhere.

I turn on the coffee maker and find my place at the kitchen table. *Washington Post* for May 30th, 2015. Now there's a year straight out of *The Twilight Zone*. Some future we got though, huh? Last I looked cars still have wheels and the coffee pot still takes forever to gurgle full.

Somebody blew himself up in a crowd somewhere in the Middle East based on the dusty front page photo. Whole part of the world's shot to hell, if you ask me. Long as Saddam's still in power. Don't get Mary started though—she'll talk your ear off with her hippy crap. *We're lucky—and you KNOW it—that Drew got back from the Gulf so quick. If it turned into something bigger he could have come home dead or in a wheelchair.*

What did he expect when he enlisted—a paid vacation?

The phone rings on the kitchen counter. Or beeps, rather. They don't ring anymore.

"Yes?"

"Dad, you're up."

"I am."

"You take your pills?"

Drew always sounds older on the phone. Like the way I sound on home movies, talking back to me.

"Why would I do that," I say.

Drew breathes into the phone. Either that or he's outside, a phone booth with a door that won't latch.

"Do you remember what we talked about yesterday?" Drew says.

Of course I do. It was colder than today. The kitchen tiles froze my barefeet. Today it's all sticky and warm. Leave it to my brother to call me just when the pipes have iced over. *Fucking blizzard outside and all you want to do is drink. What would I tell Mary? Oh, Mary, Brent's on another bender and he wants me put the chains on the tires so I can buy him his next whiskey.*

"Are you drinking again?" I say.

"What?" he says.

"How much have you had, Brent." The floor's still sticky, like someone's poured his flask out over it.

It takes him a minute to say anything but I can still hear the wind.

"Dad, you didn't take them, did you."

"Take who?"

"Never mind. I'm on my way over." He starts laughing. "I don't know if you're lying, if you can't remember, or both. But I'll tell you it's getting pretty old having this conversation every morning."

He hangs up. I would have done it first if he didn't beat me to it. The hell's he calling me a liar for.

Is it just me or did dial tones used to be louder?

The coffee's too bitter. I reach in the fridge for some milk, and there's a picture of her on the door. 1942-2010.

Sometimes I remember things and it fills me like a bucket.

I sit at the kitchen table and drink my coffee and it tastes a little sour now. A splotch of it falls onto the newspaper, smudging a headline. Looks like somebody blew himself up somewhere in the Middle East.

The calendar says July 4th and my car's gone. Or, rather, now it's enormous and was made in Japan, and Drew's getting out of it.

"What did you do with it?" I say.

"Happy fourth, Dad." He hugs me. I swear he didn't have that bald spot last time I saw him. Must be those cell phones, all the radio waves melting the hair away like chemo. *I'm not afraid of it, Richie—and maybe it will work. On the bright side my showers will be a lot shorter and you won't have to snake the drain anymore.*

"What did you do with my car?" I say.

"We're not talking about this again." He opens the passenger side door like a horny prom king. "Hop on in."

"Where we going?" I say. "I'll drive."

"I got some fireworks from Pennsylvania for the kids and we're setting them off in the backyard. They'll be excited to see you."

Guy at the plant lost his fingers that way. He didn't tell management because he thought he'd get fired. He wore a black glove on his left hand and the fingers just hung there limp while he monitored the liquid steel transfer. Went on for months. The bosses only found out when he got into a fist fight with Harper and turned out to be missing a fist. Then they fired him. *You should have seen it, Mary. He tore off his glove and it was like he just peeled off his hand.*

Drew drives too fast. No way he'll pass the test if he keeps this up. Not to mention the air conditioning is about to frostbite my knees.

"You forgot to signal," I say. "And stop jerking the wheel so much."

"Okay, Dad."

He must be taking a back way. Don't recognize any of these streets or houses, all the same one after the other, white siding and a hoop in the driveway. Now he pulls into one of them and shuts off the engine.

"Let's go see everyone." He unbuckles his seatbelt and then his eyes meet mine, intense and blue like a wolf. "My wife Amy and my two boys Connor and Bradley." He speaks slowly, draws out each name. You'd think I'm a foreigner who needs a goddamn roadmap to understand English.

"Sure," I say. Last I saw Amy she was twenty-four with a five-month belly. I didn't know they made wedding dresses that size.

There are two teenage boys in the kitchen drinking Cokes. One of them tall with a crewcut and a Penn State cap, the other shorter, wiry, a little fuzz over his lip and a zit about to pop all over his forehead.

Drew guides me in with his hand as if I'm blindfolded. "Connor, Bradley—say hi to Grandpa."

They both mutter greetings and then make eyes at each other. Some secret language between brothers. The other day I knew Brent would end up in the drunk tank just from the way he signed his Christmas card, the upward slant of his name and the crooked penmanship. *Next time it'll be a fucking telephone pole instead of a rickety fence, and I'll be picking him up from the morgue instead of the clink. Mary? I can't hear you. Put the baby down and speak into the phone.*

Amy comes in through the sliding door with a plate of well-done hamburgers. She's thin and her skin is bronze—none of the freckles she had last time. Don't know why she didn't let me do the grilling. Mary must be out back picking her tomatoes from the garden. She's always too particular though, tossing out anything with a bruise or an odd shape. I should get her back in here before she gets lost, turning each tomato around in her fingers until she can find a reason not to serve it.

"Great to see you, Richard." Amy leans in and kisses me on the cheek without putting down the plate. "I hope you came hungry." She smells of Pert Plus. Weak water pressure and carrot-colored tiles and Mary's fingers through my hair. *Let me rinse you off since you've been so dirty.*

"No cheese?" the taller boy says.

"Grandpa's lactose intolerant," Drew says.

The taller boy burps, a mist of Coca-Cola and something else. "Are they all for him?"

"Go get the buns, smartass."

The taller boy lifts the Coke can to his lips and glugs it down. The shorter boy then quietly reaches up into a cabinet and pulls out a pack of hamburger buns. He unwraps it and hands one to me.

"You get first pick, Grandpa."

He's Drew's kid. That's right. Connor or Brent. One of them almost killed his mother, had to be ripped out, metal claws across the belly. Drew called home after he yukked due to all the blood. I could smell the vomit on his breath over the phone. *It's a boy. Amy's out cold but she's all right. Is Mom there?*

Outside a fly zips around my burger and Drew brings out a stereo and the two boys fumble with some packages out on the lawn. Burger tastes like charcoal but is somehow red on the inside. The music is loud and doesn't have any melody. Amy sits down on the bench next to me with a salad. Lettuce and fresh tomatoes all tossed in dressing, fresh tomatoes wet in the sun.

"Glad you found some you could use," I say.

"Some what?" Her voice has a smile.

"Tomatoes."

"There's a stand out on Route 1," Mary says. "Freshest I've ever found."

Drew comes over and puts his hands on her shoulders.

"She yells at me if I buy produce at the Giant. Lining the coffers of Big Agro, right babe?"

He takes a sip of Budweiser. I can see his throat pumping it downward. She puts her hand on his, as if I'm not sitting right there. Last Thanksgiving Brent grabbed her ass right in front of me in the living room, the sibling rivalry getting worse with each drink, and Mary put a finger to her mouth, their little secret. He sobered up as soon as I shoved him into the spice rack, knocking it off the wall and dusting the kitchen with cinnamon and parsley. *Touch my fiancée again and see what happens.*

"Haven't you had enough?" I snatch the beer from his hand and pour it out onto the deck. Trickling between the boards.

"What the hell, Dad?"

"It's fine." Mary gets up and straightens her blouse. "I'll get you a soda."

"He wants a drink, he can get it himself," I say. I drop the empty bottle and it rolls along the grooves.

"No, Amy—a Coke would be great." He lifts his burger to his mouth and bites nearly half of it away.

Suddenly the lawn begins to crackle. The two boys are out there laughing, lifting firecrackers up, lighting them and tossing them away. Each pop sounds like a blown tire, or a baseball bat slamming a ball into the stands, or a gunshot. When they run out of crackers they start tearing into a massive black bag at the top of the hill. Looks straight out of Chinatown—Roman candles, mortars, wicks attached to shapes I've never seen before. I'm following the glow of a lighter angling under some rocket or other when a voice flies over my shoulder.

"Not yet, boys!"

The taller boy perks his head up. "But it's getting darker now, Dad."

"That thing in the sky looks a lot like the sun to me." Drew's walking up to them now, licking ketchup off his fingers. "Come on, pack it back up until it sets."

But the tall one already lit the wick. Before his dad finishes speaking, the thing sparks and whistles and zips away into the woods. So loud Mary's bound to get an instant migraine from it.

"Get back inside now!" Drew's voice echoes around the yard.

The boys snicker their way down, brushing past me and then through the screen door. Like me and Brent when we snagged that issue of *Playboy* from the magazine stand. Fighting over girls even when they were made of paper. *Let me get a turn with it first, Rick. I swear I'll be quick.*

Amy runs up the hill and catches Drew before he comes back down. She hands him a red can and talks close to his ear. More secrets, right in front of me no less. But Brent always forgets my sharp hearing. Even whispers carry during lulls in the music, and the movement of Mary's wet lips betrays some of her coded words, the "we can afford it" and "it's what he needs." Whatever she wants he keeps shaking his head, pushing back. The red can hangs unopened between a couple fingers. He uses the word "depressing." Then he glances in my direction and sees me watching.

"Your burger cooked enough, Dad?" he calls.

"Haven't had one yet," I say. "But don't worry. I know what you're up to."

They turn to each other—the punctuation at the end of a secret talk—and then walk over hand-in-hand to sit at the picnic table. Whatever they were planning, it looks like they left a whole haul of explosives at the top of the hill.

The calendar says August 1st. It's dark out and I'm watching some show where a serial killer carves his initials into his victims' faces and then leaves them on park benches or in movie theaters. Mary's up on the mantle. The TV flickers against the urn like a distant storm. She loves shows like this. Can always guess who did it in the first ten minutes. Maybe she just pays closer attention—I already forget some of the clues. Wherever she is now, she's got this one pegged for sure.

A weird whooshing sound murmurs under the show's soundtrack. The camera zooms in real close to everyone who talks. Like Brent with his home movies, right up in your face and calling out drunken stage directions. *Tell us how it feels to be fifty, Rick. Give us a thumbs up if you like being fifty. What's it feel like to be fifty? Get Mary over here. Give him fifty kisses for the camera. One, two, three . . .*

A commercial starts for some pill that gives you a hard-on. Asking men to admit their darkest secret to a pharmacist. At the plant tomorrow Harper will tell me about how long he lasted with Linda and I'll try to one-up him with the time that

Mary and I made love after the power went out, and we'll both skip the part where we had to tug on ourselves for ten minutes to even get going. Like starting a car in the winter.

There's a weird whooshing sound in this commercial. But when the next one starts, the sound keeps going. It's coming from down the hall.

Drew must have stopped up the toilet again. The kid eats like a pig and shits like one too. *Military might help you lose a few pounds at the very least. Hey, I'm just being honest with him, Mary, no need to go soft.*

The lid's closed but there's water pouring out from all sides. Son of a bitch. It sloshes around my feet and up to the cuffs of my pajamas. I lift the plunger from behind the tank and I open the lid.

Somebody tried to flush the *Washington Post* down the toilet. It's rolled up like a fly swatter and lodged right into the hole, little clumps of paper floating around in the yellow water like jellyfish. Sickly yellow water. *It's a sign that your brother's liver has shut down.*

I don't want to see it. Enough of Brent's mess. I go around the corner to the living room, tracking wet footprints on the carpet and humping the plunger over my shoulder. The phone feels heavy tonight and the keys stick too long after I press them.

To see him poisoned like that, Mary, I don't know what the fuck to do. I can't shake the color of his face. I thought their job was to fix that with makeup. How long do we have to stay here? I already paid my respects.

They're putting a wide-eyed old man in handcuffs, the credits are starting to roll, and someone's knocking on my door. The clock says eleven. No time of night for a friendly visit. The closest thing for me to grab is a plunger, of all things.

"Dad?"

"Who is it." Both hands on the plunger.

"It's Drew." He peeks his head through the crack. "I brought my toolbox."

"I've never seen you hold so much as a screwdriver."

I let him in. His shoes mush into the carpet, all damp. Why buy a welcome mat if nobody ever uses it?

"Jesus, how long has it been running?" He dips away down the hall, sloshing with each step. I hadn't noticed until now how cold and wet my feet are.

Mary will have a fit when she sees this. The beige carpet soaked to deep brown, the water stains along the walls, the smell of piss. And now what looks like a newspaper, all rolled up and decayed, being tossed out into the middle of the floor. Drew follows it out of the bathroom, his sleeves folded back and the hair up to his elbows wet and black against his arms.

"How did this happen?" he says.

"You better think of a good excuse to tell your mother."

"I won't have to." His voice gets louder. "But I can't trust you by yourself anymore."

"You take a three month vacation to Iraq and suddenly you know what's best for everybody." *Don't talk to him like that, Richie. Our son's grown a lot in the past year. He'll be a father soon.*

His face wrinkles in a way I haven't seen before. More lines than I remember, and a weariness to his eyes. When did my son become a man?

"We're not doing this again." He throws open the linen closet and starts pulling towels out and onto the floor. "Put that plunger down and help me clean this up."

"It's time you learn to clean up your own messes," I say, handing the plunger out to him. "You need it more than I do."

The calendar says September 14th and there's a black woman at the kitchen counter. I've never seen her before but she's smiling at me and organizing pills into weekly containers. Mary always has old friends sprouting out of nowhere, and I'm supposed to pretend I know them.

"How do you know Mary again?" I say.

"I wish I had." She almost sings when she talks, and almost dances as she pours the tablets into her hand and separates them. "She's so beautiful in all your pictures."

Once the hair started going Mary didn't take any pictures. That year's been erased from the family record. And I'll be damned but I can't remember her hair ever coming back.

"Did Mary have her hair last you saw her?" I say.

The woman clicks the last compartment shut and shakes the whole week. Sounds like seven rattlesnakes.

"Such stunning red hair," she says. "You were a lucky man to snatch her up."

Brent always said that too. He'd be in his garage buffing the headlights and going on about my girl as if I'd stolen her from somebody. *A regular guy like you nabs a girl like that, you have no choice but to lock her down. You pop the question yet, or do I have to do it for you?*

My favorite story to tell Drew is that she proposed to me. Right after Brent tried and got turned down. Later he blamed it on the drink. My brother was the drink.

But I didn't steal her—she doesn't belong to anybody.

"Do you know where she went?" I say. I don't hear the blow dryer or the TV or the shower and the only perfume I smell is this woman's, harsher than Mary's. Usually she's down here with scrambled eggs on the skillet and her crossword puzzle sprawled open on the table. *What's an eight letter word for dusk? See any words like that in the Sports section?*

"I'm sure she'll be back soon," the woman says. "In the meantime, I brought something new we can work on."

The 100 pieces sound like poker chips as they crumble out of the box. It's an alpine scene with a cabin at the base of a mountain.

"I don't do puzzles," I say.

"Sure you do." The woman is already sifting through the pieces, finding the corners. "Last week we did the space shuttle, remember?"

She's lying. Something's going on here. Did Mary lock up her jewelry before she left? I can't remember the last time I saw my wallet.

"I want you to leave." I stand up from the table and the slick linoleum almost makes me slide to the floor. "I don't know who you are."

"Sure you do, Mr. Rick." She doesn't look up from the puzzle pieces. "I'm Angelina, remember? Your son Drew introduced us two weeks ago and we've been getting to know each other ever since."

"So Drew sent you?" I walk over to the phone. It's hard to move fast. "Does Mary know about this?"

"She knows I'm here to help," Angelina says.

Is it just me or did dial tones used to be louder? I enter Drew's number and it starts to ring.

"Is Drew there?"

"Hi Richard." It's a woman. "Are you having a good Saturday?"

"Who's this?"

"It's Amy. Give me just a minute and I'll fetch Drew."

I wait with the silence in my ear. I watch a black woman I've never seen before shifting puzzle pieces around my kitchen table. I focus on her hands—there's something soothing about them. They move in circles, catching some pieces with the undersides of the palms and leaving other pieces behind. After a few cycles a pattern starts to form, greener pieces in the bottom half and bluer pieces in the top. With each sweep the hands bring just a little more order to the clutter of the table. Mary always clears the table, takes a special pride in seeing it empty after being so full of dishes and crumbs and silverware just moments before. *I love you to pieces, but when I'm gone you'll need a Hazmat team to clean the kitchen every night.*

Cold hands, her head as bare and cratered as the December moon through the hospital window.

I've started to cry. I don't know why the phone is up to my ear, broadcasting silence, but I hang it up and sit down at the table. The woman smiles and clicks a couple pieces together. I dig both hands into the pile. I think I've found a corner we can work our way out from.

GETTING OVER IT

SHEILA BLACK

Consider it a lesson—here is how
you make soup. It is like the stars—a broth

of ghosts and bone. It is good to inhale

the steam that rises from the pot, the rich
mulch of long fallow, long

gone. In the mirror a winkle cuts
my face in two.

I don't care, don't even pine.
I get out the clean cutting board

and chop an onion into tiny squares.

I look as if I have been frowning a long time.

I know you were the last one—

the way a person might have one bird
for a whole season—

a dove that cries in a peculiar way or
the cardinal flashing just now outside a window.

I turn up the flame and the onions brown.

The broth is better if it tastes a little burned—

darkness and what light we make of it,

like those funny pictures of bone in which
the bones appear to shine, which is only a

trick of radium—that dangerous, but beautiful element
one would never put in soup,
and the woman who plunged her hands

into it until her skin peeled off,

until she was possessed by a truly terrible

weariness. She wanted to know—the way

love would amortize every butterfly,

would pin it to a sky of blue velvet and

will it to fly even into winter.

CONCERNING A RIGHT DEVOTION

JEFF HARDIN

to Darnell Arnoult

This voice—I grant it may be mine,
though if you need it for your own,
I will grant it to you; if yours is
lonely, grieved, weakened by this
brutal world, our voices together
can wander along, inspecting
the presence of leaves drifting
on a mountain stream the town's
center keeps a secret. I believe
in providence—perhaps I should
say this voice believes—for it goes
ahead of me, preparing a way.
I follow. And always I'm uncertain
where we're being summoned to,
but if it invites into ourselves
the wakening of blooms each April
along a woods line of dogwoods,
then I'll agree that more is happening
to us than we deserve, more than
we invent on our behalf. I hold
that we should whisper words
into the lives of others, though I'm
not prepared to say which ones
will lead us where we need to go.
Alive could be a start. Or *winter
light.* Or *lingering.* I love the word

allegiance for its invitation to
a faithfulness that says that each
is an homage to who another might
become if only each could find
the right devotion. Yes, at least
for now we share this earth, we
share that we can share a voice,
and what in its becoming it becomes
will take us both to hear, to follow
where its slightest shadows slide
above the darker stones and stems
lying all around us in an age
where maps have lost their way.

FIDEL AND THE REVOLUTION

CARL AUERBACH

I would like to write a poem, Fidel,
that would serve your revolution,
but I find myself unable.
All that I can do, Fidel, is to write a poem
about how I try to write a poem
that would serve your revolution.

In the first verse I start to write, Fidel,
that I still remember Martha, my first girlfriend
back in college; how she'd walk barefoot on the lawn
from her dorm room to the commons, treading carefully
so as not to crush the soft grass and the flowers;
how proud I was of her when she went to Cuba
to cut cane with the first brigade, the Venceremos,
how much respect I had for her when she returned,
dropped out of school, and went to work to serve the people
at a clinic in el Barrio de Harlem.

But then I have to write, in a second verse, Fidel,
that I can't forget how Martha wept and wept—
I thought she'd never stop—when she learned about
the dissidents that your soldiers put in prison,
and her outrage at your claim that this was done
to save the revolution; how she went back to school
to study corporate law; how shocked I was
to hear that she died when her car went off
the road, which her parents called an accident,
but I knew was suicide.

And so the darkness of the second verse
blots out the brightness of the first,
and I erase them both.

So I start to rewrite the first verse, Fidel,
write this time about Marisol, an old woman
in Havana, about my anger when I heard about her life
under Batista; how she stood outside the iron gates
of a mansion in Vedado and begged for food,
wearing dirty rags that did not cover up
what she called her private parts; about the joy I felt
when she told me that the revolution taught her
how to read and write, gave her work and dignity,
and for a moment, Fidel, I believed in you.

But then a second verse arrives, Fidel,
about my father who once dreamed of revolution—
he named me Carl Fredrick Auerbach,
after Karl Marx and Freidrich Engels—
about his bitter voice when he spoke about
Stalin's gulags, Khrushchev's revelations;
about the scorn he heaped upon his younger self,
and I hear his advice to me before he died:
to trust no one and to believe in nothing,
and I feel ashamed, Fidel, of my belief in you.

And so the new life in the first verse
is aborted in the second
and I leave them both unwritten

I would like write a poem, Fidel,
that would serve your revolution,
but I find myself unable.

All that I can do, Fidel, is to write this poem
about why I can not write a poem
that would serve your revolution.

MEMORIES OF A TIME AND PLACE

ORMAN DAY

February and April 1967—San Francisco

From a speech by Gov. Ronald Reagan before the California
Newspaper Publishers Association, a few of us college editors
from Los Angeles venture into the night hoping to encounter
hippies a few weeks after we saw published photos of stoned
revelers at the first "Human Be-In, A Gathering of Tribes." Not
far from Haight-Ashbury, we find the Blue Unicorn coffee
house. It's closed for business, but we're let inside by Barbara, a
hippie chick who gives us free coffee, which we sip beneath a
big image of Malcolm X. Afterwards, Barbara and her long-
haired boyfriend lead us to their commune. The guy whispers,
"Walk real quiet up the stairs because a lot of people are on
trips now. If you make too much noise, they may think you're
plainclothesmen."

Their garret flat is bare of everything but bed springs (no
mattress) and a red lightbulb at the ceiling. A couple living in
the commune is planning to marry, Barbara tells us, and is
going to pass out LSD sugar cubes to their guests.

The next night my friend Baxter—a conservative Republican
from Altadena—and I enter the Avalon Ballroom, where
Country Joe and the Fish, Sparrow and Kaleidoscope are playing psychedelic music as strobe lights flicker, the ceiling pul-
sates with blobs of color, and my striped tie glows in the
ultraviolet light. I twirl my key chain while swaying and

spinning, the lights making me feel bodiless, surrounded by hundreds of other dancers without partners. Though I've never smoked pot or even drunk a beer and I'm wearing a dress shirt and slacks, I'm part of this massive organism afire with spectral-looking vests, flowing dresses, flowers, beads, headbands, and granny glasses. I wave Baxter toward the pandemonium of the dancefloor, but he refuses to move from the dimly lit sidelines, afraid the strobes and hypnotic music will cause him to lose his sanity and self-control.

A hippie chick asks me to smell her dying rose, and I inhale and smile. She tells me she was kicked out of junior college because her nursing instructor told her to either cut her long blonde hair or get out. She got out, and now she paints the air for me with graceful movements of her head.

Two months later with reporter's notebook in hand, I return to San Francisco in a chartered bus bearing fellow Cal State L.A. students who'll march in a massive parade protesting the Vietnam War. I'm a lukewarm supporter of America's role in the conflict, but I help carry my schoolmates' "End The War Now" banner to record cheers and ridicule along the route. For the school paper, I'll write, "A cute wisp of a girl in tight, black pants and sweater had a sign—sewn onto the back of her upper garment—that read, 'Get out of Vietnam and into something cute.'"

That night I dance at the Avalon to music by groups I've never heard of: The Doors and the Steve Miller Blues Band. For hours, I weave through the flickering light, but I can't find the girl with the dying rose. At 2 a.m., Ron—another *College Times* reporter—and I thumb to the Haight in search of a free crash pad. At a creaky Victorian house, we're led to a cold basement full of curled sleepers by members of the Diggers, anarchy's version of the Salvation Army. I step behind the hunk of cardboard that serves as the door to the bathroom. Since the water system's decrepit, only every tenth person is supposed to flush the besplattered toilet. I'm grateful I can stand because I'm No. 9.

April 1974—Calgary, Canada

When you're home in West Covina, an unanswered phone is just a minor disappointment. But when you're on the road and your body's rancid with sweat and other people's cigarette smoke, it can turn the pack on your back into a granite slab headed for the top of an Egyptian pyramid. So after two nights and three days on Greyhound buses, my clothes doused with aftershave, my chin unshaven, I dial the number of John, a former high school classmate, the only person I know in Calgary. My body sags against the booth when no one answers.

In a drizzle dappling my wire-rimmed glasses, I meander with no particular destination from the bus terminal toward what I guess is the center of downtown. Along the way, I check prices at motels, but they're too steep for my budget.

Then I stop myself. I didn't worry when I hopped an eastward-bound freight train out of L.A. five years ago and rolled into New Orleans with a couple bucks in my pockets and no place to stay. Now I'm relatively rich because I've got a Greyhound pass and a few hundred dollars in my jeans. Isn't uncertainty one of the lures of travel? Where's my faith in the Cosmos?

Within a minute, a young Chinese-Canadian woman calls to me from the steps of a beauty salon. Maureen asks if I need a free place to stay. Yes. She directs me to a commune run by Jesus People. Maybe she'll see me there later.

Humming Handel's Hallelujah Chorus, I stride toward the church. Within a few blocks of the commune, I wait at a signal and notice a woman smiling at me from the opposite corner. Long brown hair topped by a knit cap. Dimpled cheeks. Bra-less beneath her sweater. When the light changes,

I stand still. When she passes, I ask, "Can I buy you some coffee?"

She stops, turns to face me and says, "No, but I'll buy you some."

The Lord works in strange ways, I think, although the Jesus People would've blamed my detour on the Devil because Valerie works as a topless dancer. In a tavern, she teaches me to play electronic darts and then beside our table, to slow music from a combo, we brush our teasing bodies against each other until the manager warns us both dancing and hugging are forbidden in his establishment. Properly seated again, we invite James to move to our table. He's eighteen and wants to meet girls, but says he's too shy. I counsel James to forget his pride and take risks, citing my own encounter with Valerie as an example. He acts on my advice immediately: every time I leave for the restroom to try to unplug my bowels after days on the bus, James lists reasons why Valerie should ditch me for him.

Before searching for a cheap motel with Valerie, I make one last call to John. He's home, his family's away in Boston, and we're invited to sleep on a mattress on his basement floor. During a late-night conversation, Valerie listens raptly to my story about my appearance as Super Frog on *Let's Make a Deal*, a TV show she never misses. I won a motorboat in October 1972, and I still haven't received it. Not long ago, the dealer told me my boat was nearly ready, so I quit my job as a railroad carpenter and prepared to sell my prize and travel around the world. Hearing nothing but excuses from the dealer, I finally had to get away from the family home, so I bought a bus pass. And here I am.

The next afternoon, Valerie and I share a moment of lyrical beauty. She and I are entranced listening to John practice on his cello for a concert that night . . . and suddenly just outside the picture window . . . lacy snowflakes scurry and flutter and swirl . . . as if they're notes of the sonata, plucked and bowed in the heavens.

In the morning, Valerie and I hug each other a long time in the terminal. Reluctantly she's leaving behind our laughter and confessional conversations, and returning to a distant city and a jealous boyfriend. After she leaves my life, I stare at the departure board. With my bus pass in hand, I board the very next bus. It's taking me west to Vancouver. But I'm growing weary of schedules, and I'll soon be standing at the side of a road with my thumb out, in search of the unexpected.

June 1974—Finland and Soviet Union

In the Helsinki station, my girlfriend Carol and I eat a half-liter of orange-vanilla ice cream with wooden spoons, blissful in each other's company after the sometimes turbulent days we spent traveling in Europe and North Africa. Inside the train, I lean out an open window to touch fingertips and say, "I love you," as tears feather from the corners of my eyes.

I'm alone in my compartment until a group of Finnish teachers clamber aboard, on their way to Russia for a drunken holiday. Already festively inebriated, the men call me "California" and share their food and vodka with me. They beam with pleasure when I praise the Finnish sauna. "First," I say, "I got in very, very hot water . . . " Vigorously they nod their heads. " . . . then I jumped in very, very cold water . . . " They nod their heads. " . . . and then I took off my clothes." Their faces freeze and then they burst out laughing.

In Leningrad outside the Peter Paul Fortress, I join Russians who sunbathe during their lunch breaks by standing in front of a wall. Taking off my shirt, I stand between a man in briefs and a blonde in a two-piece suit, and am surprised by the intensity of the reflected heat. Nearby, young people bat a volleyball in a circle. No laughter. No words. No transistor radios. Only the thump of fists.

A German tourist named Christiane leads me around Moscow, showing me a chandeliered metro and the GUM department store. I notice Russian clothing varies in style from halfway modern to Depression breadline. On the street, a man offers to buy my threadbare jacket. I consider for a moment before realizing I'd find it difficult to spend the rubles since the Russian demand my hard currency for everything I want to buy, except ice cream.

For the first leg of my journey aboard the Trans-Siberian Railway, I share my second-class compartment (two lower and two upper berths) with Hans and Peter, Swiss backpackers. One afternoon in the dining car, we're joined by boisterous Russian men who buy us wine and sing folk tunes for us. To return their hospitality, we give them American chewing gum (worth a dollar a pack on the black market) and a few ballpoint pens, a luxury because Soviet pens leak. We think we're being generous, but their leader demands more presents. We laugh and excuse ourselves. Before they can follow us to our compartment, the conductor discovers they have no tickets. As they're put off the train, someone calls after them, "Hooligans!"

Because I drink copious amounts of tea brewed by the car's samovar, I frequently utilize the lavatory, which has a Western-style toilet. Once, while I'm waiting outside, the restroom door swings open. Inside is a man who's apparently used to dropping his pants over a hole in the ground because he's squatting with his feet on the seat while the train bounds down the tracks. If I could speak Russian, I'd commend him on his balance and suggest he go surfing in the Sea of Okhotsk.

After spending a night in Irkutsk, I board a train alone for the three-day ride to Khabarovsk and discover I'm the only non-Soviet in my car. My bunkmates are two Russians in their twenties like me. Nicholas is a scientific researcher on his way to northeast Siberia. Lara's a university student who shares her name with the heroine of Boris Pasternak's *Dr. Zhivago*. Lara's got curly brown hair, sensitive eyes, a clear doll-like face. Her beauty makes me want to howl wolf-like from the steppes. For some reason, I assume she and Nicholas are lovers.

Using Nicholas's smattering of English, sign language and drawings, we manage to communicate, although we can't exactly discuss the symbolism in Pushkin's poetry. He tells me the Soviet Union is the freest country in the world, and he can travel anyplace he wants if he has the money. I try to explain that his government deliberately makes it too expensive for its citizens to travel outside the Soviet Block. In response, he can't believe I financed my trip by working as a railroad carpenter. Periodically we pass female railway workers shoveling ballast under the rails and it's obvious they can't afford to vacation in Greece.

The fourth berth is eventually taken by Tanya from Georgia, a Soviet republic that Nicholas and Lara frown upon as backward. Tanya's a brunette who's garbed like many other passengers in a sweat suit. I can't eat enough dining car meals to use up all of my food coupons, so I exchange them for wine for the four of us. Though we kiss a bit with wine on our lips, Tanya appears to be puritanical.

I discern a similarity between patriotic Soviet women like her and Christian fundamentalists. Both groups dislike long hair on men, rock music, free love and criticism of their beloved government. One group worships God; the other bows before Vladimir Lenin, whose glass-encased embalmed corpse I would've viewed in Moscow but for the renovation of Red Square.

Before I disembark in Khabarovsk, I pose the three of them for a photo in the doorway of the compartment. Nicholas and Tanya angle toward the camera. Apart from the others, smiling beatifically, Lara faces me straight on, as if she's staring deep into my soul and doesn't want me to ever forget her. Hoisting my bag to my shoulder after clicking my camera, I shake

Nicholas' hand. Tanya nods her head. I turn to Lara and she winks at me. Sensually.

After I develop my slides, I hold the one of the three of them up to the sun. I realize now what I didn't realize then: Lara isn't Nicholas' lover and if I had stretched my hand toward her berth during the dark of night, she might have found it and caressed it.

May 1980—India

In her office in Upper Dharamshala, a Tibetan doctor pulls gumdrop-sized herbal pills from jars stretched across six shelves. She promises they'll cure both my nearsightedness and spreading baldness. Although they present the possibility of returning to Orange County with hair and without glasses, the pills are horrid-tasting and hard to swallow even when I halve them. So when my stomach turns tumultuous with Delhi Belly a few days later, I toss the pills out a bus window. As I joke to friends later, "I prefer to recede and squint than retch and sprint."

August 1984—Guatemala

In a tavern in Antiqua, a city of old ruins sitting below a volcano, I listen to a story told by Robert, a thin man from San Francisco.

Boarding a bus in El Salvador, Robert took a seat at the front and a Swiss woman friend sat at the back. During the ride, a Salvadoran *hombre* leaned against his friend, so Robert squeezed between them. The *hombre* leaned against Robert, who reacted with mild displeasure. Then the *hombre* brought out a hand grenade, and several times pretended to pull its pin and said, "Ka-pow," flinging out his hands. Robert decided to laugh along, but he grew concerned when the *hombre* pretended to explode the grenade near some children. Robert told his friend in English that if the man pulled the pin, there would be eight seconds for her to break the window and for him to grab the grenade and throw it outside. Finally, in Spanish, Robert told the *hombre* he must think he was a big man because he had a grenade. The hombre denied this vehemently, put away the grenade, set his head against Robert's shoulder and dissolved into tears. Robert stroked his head. At the next stop, the *hombre* got off the bus

When Robert finishes his story, I know I have to go to El Salvador. Civil war or not.

August 1984—El Salvador

During my five days in the country, I never see another American or European. This isn't reassuring, nor is the rubble left by civil war. Every time my bus crosses a bridge, I hold my breath. As in Guatemala, my rides are frequently interrupted by military checkpoints, where soldiers frisk us and study our identification. Healthy young men are instantly drafted into the army and forced to board a truck waiting to take them to basic training to learn how to hunt revolutionaries in the lush mountains.

These rebels, I'm warned, sometimes stop buses on the Pan America Highway and ask passengers–particularly *gringos*–to donate to their war chest. Then they torch the bus and one has the perverse pleasure of watching one's backpack go up in flames. I like to travel light, but not that light.

August 1984—Nicaragua

Just inside the country, I edge my way into a small bus so crowded the fare collector has to crawl across the roof and reach his head and arm through the window to collect tickets. Later, waiting in a village terminal for a larger but no less crowded bus to Managua, the capital, I'm surprised to see Bo, my Swedish friend. Since we parted at the Guatemala-El Salvador border, he's been traveling with a Marxist from Northern California. We're joined by a German doctor helping the

Sandinista government.

In Managua, Bo and I are surprised to see hundreds of Americans and Europeans here to support the revolution. Walls everywhere are adorned with stenciled silhouettes of Augusto Cesar Sandino, who rebelled against U.S. occupation of his country from 1927-1933 and then in 1934 after the Americans withdrew, was assassinated by National Guard forces led by Gen. Anastasio Somoza Garcia, who grabbed power two years later.

I express my dismay so many of the visiting radicals spend time loafing in the posh Intercontinental Hotel, a place a *campesino* can't begin to afford. I also question claims made by Marxist supporters that the Sandinistas had turned the country into something of a proletarian paradise free of crime and inequality.

The German tells us flatly that unlike other Central American countries, Nicaragua has no beggars. The next day the doctor, Bo and I are walking near an earthquake-leveled church when we're asked for money by two girls, one with a severely burned face. I tell *Herr Doktor*, "I guess that shoots your idea that there are no beggars here." He answers that the girls are only playing.

The next day, Bo and I are asked for a contribution by a man missing a leg. After giving the man a few coins, I tell Bo, "There's another person pretending to be a beggar."

These, though, are the only beggars I see here. In other Latin American countries, I rarely eat a meal without someone eyeing my plate. Children often ask for my chicken bones so they can suck out the marrow.

Because I changed ten dollars at the black market rate before entering the country, I possess enough cordobas to pay for nine meals, including several at the Intercontinental and McDonald's. As a show of solidarity with the revolution, Bo had been convinced by his Marxist companion to change his money at the official rate. Consequently Bo's meals and ice cream cones cost eight times as much as mine. I cackle every time a check's delivered to our table.

Nicaragua's not as inexpensive as it could have been, though, because "dirty capitalists" demand American dollars for my hotel cubicle and bus ticket to Costa Rica.

September 1984—Ecuador

Even though he knows that most of them don't like to be photographed, Martin—my Swiss traveling partner—surreptitiously takes pictures of Indians at their open-air market in Otavalo. Sitting in front of a large building away from the market, Martin turns his telephoto lens towards a baby suckling at its mother's breast. Angered, an Indian man urinates so the liquid streams downhill. After snapping several pictures, Martin touches the damp seat of his trousers. He possesses a Leo's outsized pride, so—suppressing cackles and chortles that want to rise to my lips—I hold my belly as tight as I can.

October 1984—Peru

After an inspection's completed at a military checkpoint in the Andes, a dozen soldiers—their faces hidden behind ski masks and their arms cradling machine guns—follow us passengers onto our bus. A fair distance before the next village, they're let out to encircle some primitive one-story buildings. By the time I finish eating breakfast in a rustic café, soldiers are storming a small house to capture a member of *Sendero Luminoso*, the Shining Path, a Maoist revolutionary group known for terrorizing those who disagree with them, including peasants, labor unionists and political leaders.

Outside our idled bus, we passengers watch a blindfolded captive being led toward a cluster of rocks until soldiers wave their guns and order us to reboard the bus if we value our lives. Inside, the bus smells as usual of flatulence, orange peels and body odor, but no one risks opening a window. Our driver tells us the young man's going to be shot to death because he won't reveal the whereabouts of other revolutionaries. As we pass a small house, on the porch stands a bewildered old man, his high forehead furrowed and his hands clasped in supplication against his sunken chest.

May 1985—China

Having sampled guinea pig in Colombia, I don't find it necessary to eat its Chinese rodent relative, the bamboo rat. But I do amuse Babs, a fellow backpacker, by sharing an obvious propaganda piece in the English-language, government-sanctioned *China Daily*.

"Rats—the number one enemy of China's farmers—are becoming top sellers in rural markets because of their 'delicious taste,'" I read aloud. "A young man who has been bringing more than a dozen 'kicking rats' to the market every other day said he sold his catch as quickly as 'hot cakes.'"

After describing the traditional rat-cooking recipe, the article reports that rat skin has become a popular material for making children's shoes because of its fine grain, flexibility, and glossy texture. A government organization urges the populace to rid the country of three to four billion rats by eating them. I tell Babs, it'll never work, because if people start paying for rats, then other people are going to start breeding them. Communist state or not.

September 2013—United States

Though we're going on the road, no one's going to mistake us for Jack Kerouac and Neal Cassady. At the wheel is Veera, age 33, a vegetarian, non-smoking, non-boozing, Hindu, computer programmer from India. His trusty sidekick is a paunchy 67-year-old with tufted gray hair and a beard, living off Social Security after working in journalism and P.R. in California. On his road trips, Kerouac motored down the highway in a '49 Hudson Commodore sedan. In North Carolina, I climb into Veera's aging gray Honda Civic. He and a bunch of other Indian guys working in IT used to play tennis with me five or so nights a week at the Durham apartment where we lived, but we've all scattered now, so this is a back-slapping reunion.

The Civic's crammed with Veera's possessions because he's finally joining his wife Raji in San Jose. After their arranged marriage was conducted in Hyderabad a couple years ago, he wanted her to move to Durham, but she refused to relocate from California. Finally his employer's letting him work from his new distant home.

Later, I learn Veera figures our trip will last a week at most, but I have other plans, though certainly not detailed ones, because my credo's taken from Kerouac: "There is nowhere to go but everywhere."

Our first night we stop at Blowing Rock in the Blue Ridge Mountains. Since my folk-singing partner Rich and I thumbed through this area in 1970 during a 100-day journey around the country, I reminisce about our experience in nearby Spruce Pine. A teenaged girl named Lola heard us performing for hamburgers and fries in a café, followed us to a bowling alley, and then invited us to sleep at her grandparents' farm. Naturally, her grandma was too frightened to open her door at night to two strangers. Lola threatened to kick open the door and whup her grandma, so the wizened old woman had no choice but to let us in. The next morning Granny taught me to milk a cow. Veera laughs and laughs at my saga.

As a freight train passes us, I describe the adrenalin rush of hopping a moving boxcar, knowing you can lose your legs if your fingers slip. In Springfield and New Salem, Illinois, I relate stories of Abraham Lincoln, my lifelong idol. We stare out at the moonlit Mississippi in Hannibal, Missouri, and I tell him about the two months I paddled the river, fighting off flies that gnawed my bare legs when eddies tried to suck my canoe into a swirling abyss.

We never once turn on the radio during our trip because Veera always has another question to ask about women (he never dated during his bachelor days and knows nothing of the female mind), life's lessons and my travels. I coach him to be a Macho Macho Man who never forgets his A-B-Cs: Always Be Cool. My mind possesses a thousand travel and newspaper stories (like the one I wrote about a talking cat), and he wants to hear them all. One difficulty: my left ear's my bad one and I keep saying, "Huh?"

A trip-long trend begins our first full day: if you don't know where you're going, it's easy to get lost, as we discover circling around Gatlinburg, Tennessee before we wonder why we've even come here. If there's a straight path somewhere, we never manage to find it, even as I carefully lift the map close to my glasses. Also, at night every road or highway in our path is under construction, creating a hallucinatory obstacle course of flashing lights, cones, and reflective barriers, bringing to mind a whipsawing attraction at Disneyland: Mr. Toad's Wild Ride.

Even more disturbing, Veera incessantly steers his Civic onto warning strips on both sides of the road, largely because he drives way too fast. So I don't protest when an Iowa state trooper tickets Veera for speeding. Now my voice carries more authority when I announce every approaching speed limit sign. Ever on the alert, I'm too afraid to take a nap.

Once he recognizes our route is circuitous, Veera doesn't dare tell his parents we're not making a quick dash across the continent because they'd think he's wasting precious time. Though fueled by strawberry-flavored tea and a salty snack of deep-fried gram flour and dried fruit instead of cheap booze and potent reefer, we're experiencing Kerouac's words: "It's an anywhere road for anybody anyhow."

For two weeks, Veera savors every moment of freedom

before he assumes the mantel of familial responsibility. We hike through the dank labyrinth of Mammoth Cave, and at the Corn Palace in Mitchell, South Dakota, eat blue popcorn while admiring murals of dyed corn, grass and grain. We sit wrapped in the mist of Idaho Falls and Old Faithful. Veera even does something he's always wanted to do: shave his head. I joke he looks like a sadhu, those itinerant holy men I saw begging and chanting in India. All he has to do now is paint his face, smoke some ganja and walk into the lobby buck naked.

And then we reach Las Vegas, where I fly back to Maryland, and Veera turns his Civic toward San Jose and his new home.

One day in 2016, I phone Veera to catch up on his life. After he quiets his two squalling children, I tell him he'll be glad to know I'll soon be wearing hearing aids I inherited from my Aunt Lucille, who just passed away at a hundred.

Recalling our adventures as we always do, Veera remembers our stay at a motel in Kentucky. At a market, I purchased a half-gallon of sumptuous lemon ice cream and stored it in the motel freezer. In the morning, I discovered the complimentary breakfast included waffles, so I brought out the ice cream. I spooned it between two waffles to create sandwiches of warmth, cold and sweetness, and served them to the motel staff. After their first bite, they grinned at the unexpected pleasure we offered them. It was a moment best described by Kerouac: "The whole universe was crazy and cock-eyed and extremely strange."

April 2015—Toledo, Spain

A cruise ship ferries my mate Debbie and me to Barcelona, where we board a bullet train for Madrid. On an excursion to Toledo, I sit on a bench watching birds nibble bread crust in the Plaza de Zocodover. Debbie's exploring shops, picking out a refrigerator magnet and gazing at the armor, shields and swords crafted from the steel for which this city is famed. I let her roam the narrow streets because—at age 69—my joints stiffen in the cold and I lose my balance if I stand still for long. I drank *cachaça* in Brazil, sake in Japan, and hard cider in Scotland, but I sense alcohol is no longer part of my travels, so I forego a pitcher of sangria. I eat a gelato cone, but I know a day of reckoning is coming soon when I'll have to monitor the level of my blood glucose.

I rode trains across America, India and Russia, so—aware of the irony—I take my seat on the trackless *tren* that will carry us tourists around the medieval city on tires bobbing on cobblestoned streets. Locals call it "the baby train," and it looks like it should transport visitors from their cars to the main gate at an amusement park. Yet, when its whistle is tooted, I'm all smiles.

DESECRATION: HOUSE, SKIN

Michele Wolf

Shaare Torah, April 2015

The swastikas speed-wheel, spinning off the walls, doors,
Windows, of my synagogue, swarm the onlookers—
Dazed, in disbelief—then etch into their skin,
Blue-inked and crackling. No bombs will blast
Today in my green neighborhood. My town will
Not host a beheading. No captured pilot will be torched
Alive inside a metal cage. We woke up to swastikas,
Spray-painted white, swirls circling the redbrick
Building—goons on camera squirting "Hitler," "KKK."

He did not return. We scrubbed down the synagogue.
Trends emerge, depart, sometimes come roaring back.
Who knew skin art would become so wildly popular?
Do you see the swastikas scrawled into my face?
The ones that crashed my home? Please, I invite
You. Please step closer. You will be better able to see.

HOMELESS GHOSTS

SUE HYON BAE

When the tv channels went off air for the afternoon,
my granny and I made up monsters.
There's an oil monster who lives on the porch.
Does it look like a clay jar? Of course, and it bounces.
But I knew we were lying, I knew she knew,
and I thought all the world knew,
that we make up and pretend to believe in stories
for the sake of storytelling. So I assumed,
when people talked about superstitions, or belief in gods,
or rites to speak to the dead, we were playing,
just as we pretend the characters on tv are real.
It was a shock to find that other children
had believed literally in Santa Claus, some grownups
believed their prayers would really be heard,
some people weren't joking when they said
they were scared of 4 or 13. And each person
had differences in belief, so that each individual
carries within an individual universe
where the facts are different from my own universe,
which isn't so universal as I had believed,
but occupied only by me. It seemed interesting
until I remembered those who refuse to leave
extra food outside the door for abandoned ghosts
who had no families to give them offerings.

Only because they didn't want strangers in the house.
It was the first time my family seemed cruel.

HAVEN'T YOU EVER WANTED TO USE THE WORD INDIGO?

LYN LIFSHIN

the way it rolls off your tongue, blue,
mysterious. It's rather old fashioned tho
but when you run out of words for the
blues, doesn't indigo give it a little
class? Then, I think of Millay with her
indigo buntings, curled on the same
velvet couches I have tho they've been
re-covered, not indigo but a chocolate
brown. One visitor stopping at Steepletop
in Edna's last years mentioned how
shabby the sofas were. I think how
Vincent gave up her velvets, lovers, drugs
for the stillness. Except for the buntings.
But I digress. Indigo. I had to listen to
The Indigo girls, found I liked their name
better. I'd like to say I found the metaphor
to cinch this poem, to pull any reader
into Indigo ecstasy when I found some
E Mail about the film Indigo Children
but when I put the name on Google,
what I read lacked all iridescent blue,
that startling hypnotic glistening. Less
there than the marine's startling icy eyes,
indigo jolting as sequins from deep under
ground as my real life pales

DIASPORA

Faith Holsaert

Our inheritance in the Diaspora is to live in this inexplicable space.
—Dionne Brand

if there was a curtain we didn't notice
if there was something other than raspberries
among dusty leaves we didn't see

we saw how the path wound up from the creek
we knew we had to carry
we knew the old man in the next town
we knew our coats smelled of pear
and our cat, we knew our cat

Maybe the portal was there all along
when we ate ramen and watched TV
    not talking   spent
    after we had danced

we are past the curtained gateway
have passed through the membrane
this end has lost the other end

we live where our memories can not
except as clearwings in their brief season
this is an inexplicable place

we had to leave our bundled words behind

the new discount words
    do not fit like our own
can someone teach us to live here

an exile is not   a guided tour
the others we think   are tourists

we grew on a soil
that fed the eyes of potatoes
that received our offered berries

Do not mistake us for
this place where we have fallen

AS THOUGH SHE COULD ACTUALLY DO SOMETHING

Nora Bonner

The Millers have lived in Bangkok for one week when Mark calls to tell Karen he has not yet left the car plant. He is three hours away, in a province called Rayong, pronounced Ra-yong or Ray-ong, Karen can't remember. He's been gone for almost four days and now he's saying that he won't make it back in time to take the kids to the Dusit Zoo like he said he would. When Karen breaks the news, Clara kicks Sam and he responds by attempting to suffocate his sister beneath a couch cushion. They serve their respected time-outs: five minutes for Clara because she is five and instigated the violence; four minutes for Sam because he is four and neglected to practice peaceful resistance. They are now flipping over the back of the couch like it's a vault.

Karen would not have let her children flip over the couch like this if they were home in Detroit. They would be climbing on their playscape in the yard and she'd be on the deck in a lawn chair, watching them over the edge of her paperback. They now live on the fourteenth floor of an apartment complex in the middle of an enormous city known for its sex trade and its prisons. They haven't been outside yet today and her children are screaming that they want to see elephants. Mark had told them that in Thailand, they'd see elephants all the time, that elephants would be everywhere; Thai people ride elephants like horses, he said. They've been in Bangkok for seven days and the only elephants the kids have seen are the plush ones Gwang and Noom gave them as welcome gifts.

Gwang and Noom Ratachanot are the only Thai people Karen knows so far by name. She knows them by default; Noom is Mark's translator, Gwang is his wife. They have a daughter, a little older than Clara, whose name Karen can't recall. It's the Thai word for pig. Gwang said it more than twice but Karen can hardly remember the Thai words for thank you or bathroom, let alone the words for barnyard animals. Gwang and her daughter have spent every day with Karen and the kids since the husbands left for Rayong. She's taken them to the Suan Lum Night Bazaar, to Chulalongkorn's Palace, and to Ocean World—the aquarium at the bottom of the Paragon Shopping Center. And though Karen feels a little guilty about it, she doesn't know what else to do but call Gwang and see if she wouldn't mind sparing another day, today, to accompany, i.e. take, the Millers to the zoo.

"I'm very sorry," Gwang says instead of saying hello, "Moo is not well."

"Is everything okay?" Karen asks this as though she could actually do something about it if everything wasn't. At her feet, Clara and Sam sit on the carpet among 64 scattered crayons, smothering an outline of Cinderella beneath thick layers of black and purple wax.

"No, not okay," Gwang says. "Moo was outside and a dog." She explains, best she can, that a strange dog came into their yard. It snagged Moo's wrist and now they were waiting for a taxi to take to the emergency room. As she listens, Karen grabs a crayon and writes Moo's name on the inside cover of Sam's Richard Scarry coloring book, noting that the Thai word for pig is the sound a cow makes. She offers to meet Gwang at the hospital but Gwang says, "I'm sorry, Karen. I know the children are boring."

"Bored," Karen says.

"I know the children are bored," Gwang says. "Maybe you can to the mall for a movie."

Going to see a movie is exactly how Karen wants to spend the afternoon. She can enjoy two hours in the dark where the people around her will stare at at the screen, not at her children and not at her. There's only one problem: "I don't know what to tell the taxi driver," she says.

"Just tell him, 'Bpai the mall.'"

Karen repeats, "Pie the mall," imagining the Novi Shopping Center covered in cream. She thanks Gwang and wishes her luck at the hospital.

"Bpai the mall," Gwang says again before they hang up.

Downstairs, Karen asks the parking attendant at their building to call a taxi while she and the children wait in the air-condi-tioned lobby. As he speaks into a walkie-talkie, the attendant cups his hand around the back of Sam's head. Karen has come to know this as the Thai version of cheek-pinching, a gesture Sam must endure from strangers whenever he goes outside. It happens to Clara too, but not nearly as much. The gestures seem kind-spirited, and she figured Sam attracted them more because he's a boy, but Noom explained to her and Mark that it was because Sam was blond, like his mother, and Clara wasn't. "From a distance," he said, "Clara looks like Thai chil-dren. You and Sam, you are the real farangs." Karen didn't know whether to blush or apologize.

Sam's reaction to this attention varies according to his mood. If he's starting his day or just had a meal, he might swat at the strangers as if they are mosquitoes. If he's due for a nap, he might growl or shout. At Ocean World, he told a woman that he was a tiger and threatened to bite off all her hair. That woman didn't understand English. This time, maybe because of his familiarity with the parking attendant, Sam merely scowls, steps back, and folds his arms over his chest.

Karen tells Sam to sit on the couch and then apologizes to the attendant that her son is so rude. The attendant smiles and says, "Never mind, Madame," followed by something in Thai. Clara stands behind him, commanding an automatic door to open and close with the wave of her arms.

When the taxi arrives, the attendant holds open the car door and the kids tumble into the back. There are no seat belts and Karen climbs into the middle so if there's an accident, she'll be the one to slam into the windshield. "Pie the mall," she says, and the driver switches on the meter. He slides into what seems at first is a traffic jam until Karen notes a red light eight or nine cars ahead. It's 1:20 p.m. on a Saturday. If she were home on a Saturday afternoon, she'd be putting away groceries or working in the garden, or talking to her sister on the phone. She usually called her sister for advice about mundane things, like how to get stains out of shirts. Who knew how long it would be before Karen could recognize the mundane things here. She'd like to talk to Angie now, but it's 1:20 a.m. in Michigan and her sister is most likely asleep.

It would be best not to talk to Angie anyway. She would ask how things are going. She'd wonder if Bangkok was still a great idea, as it was six months ago when Mark came home from the Detroit office with good news, bad news, and a set of brochures. The bad news was that the motor company no longer needed him as one of their deputy marketing directors; the good news was that Mark's boss found him a position working the same job for their office in Thailand. The brochures were of condominiums, island resorts, and weekend trekking trips through jungles. Karen had convinced Angie that Clara and Sam were still young enough to pick up a second language, and bilingual kids performed better on standardized tests. She could already picture their personal statements for college applications. On the phone, Angie would ask if the kids have picked up any Thai and Karen might have to admit that when she tried to get Clara to repeat a Thai greeting, she'd said, "Why?"

The children whine at the sight of a McDonald's near the mall's entrance and Karen reminds them that they just had lunch. Inside, they pass a waterfall display—streams trickle over a pile of what look like paper-mache rocks. Clara asks to be carried on the escalator. Sam makes the same request once he sees Karen lift his sister. Karen counts four flights to climb and then offers to carry Sam on the last two. While they ride, Karen glances at Sam to make sure he's balancing okay and realizes that the Tigers t-shirt Angie bought him is getting a little tight in the arms. She scans the second level for a children's clothing store before wondering if she, herself, would be able to fit any of the outfits in the department store windows.

As they near the fifth level, they hear what sounds like a war—cars squeal, bombs explode, and machine guns ripple in echoes. A sign overhead indicates that besides the theater, there's an arcade on that floor. "We're here to see a movie," Karen says, "Don't even ask to play those games." Her voice is lost in the noise.

They wait in line below banners advertising the latest horror movie, the printed portrait of a teenage girl with wild hair, bluish skin, and no pupils; the title, which has not been translated into English, emerges below her chest from a pool of blood. The sign behind the counter lists two children's movies among eight and Clara and Sam have seen them both: one, the latest Narnia adaptation and the other, a computer-animated version of Jack and the Beanstalk. Karen would prefer to sit through Narnia again but Clara didn't like the dragon.

At the concessions stand, Clara points to an advertisement for popcorn and demands some, which Karen buys along with a large Sprite for them to split three ways. A crowd waits out-side the theater that will show Jack and the Beanstalk. All of the benches are full. Karen sits against the wall beneath another poster advertising the same horror movie; this time, it's an old man without pupils and he holds a bloody knife. Sam stares at it. Everyone else in the lobby, as far as Karen can tell, is staring at them.

An older woman in a jean jumper comes up to Sam, points at the poster and says, "Scary?" She puts her hand on his head. Sam scowls. She doesn't go away. "Excuse me," she says, though from her pronunciation, the words sound more like accuse me. She reaches for him again and he slaps her in the face.

"No." Karen grabs his hand and yanks him to a bench that is now free. "You don't hit people."

"Ooh-wee," the woman says. She seems more amused than offended but walks away before Karen can get Sam to apologize to her.

"I hate them," Sam says, attempting to twist his arm free.

Karen sits and pulls him into her lap. "You don't hate them. You don't know them."

"I hate them."

"You hate what they do to you," she says, and bounces him on her knees. Clara sits next to her. "You can ask them to stop."

"They don't understand English," Clara says. It's a phrase she's heard many times from her mother.

"Some of them do," Karen says, cringing that she is refer-ring to Thai people as *them,* but her daughter has a point.

Clara stands on the bench and gauges the lobby. Sam stands with her, and Karen helps him balance by stretching her palm at the base of his back. With the other hand, she checks her phone and sees that Mark tried to call her an hour ago. His text message says he says he'll be home around four thirty, depend-ing on traffic, that he's sorry, and that she can try calling him back but he doesn't know if he'll have phone service on the road. He finishes by typing that he can't wait to see which panties she's wearing. This has been their joke. Every night he's guessed which pair she had on. Whether or not he guessed right, she described a new pair she pretended to have just bought from a street-vendor—a thong tied with rainbow lace or a bikini-style bottom with leopard skin print crawling up the front of her cootch. He loves it when she says the word "cootch." He doesn't answer when she tries to call him back. She texts, *Okay*. As she's putting away her phone, she notes that it's 1:47 a.m. in Detroit.

A woman in a red sundress with black polka dots and red heels stands nearby, watching her. She holds the hand of a small child in overalls; it's hard to tell if the child is a boy or a girl. The woman gestures to the empty spot on the bench next to Karen. She nods, and the woman smooths her skirt as she sits. She offers popcorn and the woman says, "No, thank you. I've eaten already," in the best English pronunciation Karen's heard since Noom.

"Where did you learn to speak like that?"

"I studied in London," she says. "Master degree."

In the next five minutes, Karen finds out the woman's name is Pun, short for Appun, which is, the woman says, the way Thai people pronounce "apple." The child is her daughter. Her name is Nok, which means bird. Karen tells her that she's just arrived from Detroit, that her husband works for a motor company and has been away in Rayong for the better part of the week, and that her children will start school next month and until then, she has no idea how she'll keep her sanity.

Pun smiles, maybe understanding. "Your children are very adorable," she says.

"Thanks."

"Especially the boy."

Karen smiles, understanding.

An usher unlocks the entrance and the crowd filters into the theater. Karen tells Pun it was nice meeting her, only then realizing that Clara is no longer by her side. She is no longer on the bench. Karen scans the lobby and finds her daughter near the theater entrance. It is not until Clara's hand is in hers that Karen realizes she'd not been breathing for the last fifteen seconds.

Once seated, they watch a preview for the horror movie from the posters; Karen guesses this as soon as an ominous pulse echoes over the speakers. Streams of blood drip into Thai script, followed by a scene in a bathroom where one man takes another man's hand, runs it under a faucet, and shoves it into an electrical socket. Clara screams.

Karen says, "Close your eyes!"

Clara climbs into Karen's lap and plugs her ears; Sam stands on his chair, also plugging his ears, and shouts that he wants to leave.

"You want to go home?"

"Yes. Now."

"Not until you finish your soda," Karen says, why, she has no idea, and grips Clara tighter. Sam sits down in a thump and wraps his mouth around the straw without using his hands, splashing Sprite on Karen's arm. Just then the entire audience, at the same time, stands from their seats.

A lone child sings over the speakers—eerie and pure—and on the screen, there's black and white footage of the Thai King standing on a balcony in front of a sea of people waving Thai flags. Some of them are smiling. Some are bewildered, as if they are watching a UFO drift down to them from the sky. His picture fades into the words: "In Remembrance of His Majesty 1927-2016"—first in English, then in Thai. The screen darkens and the audience sits.

"I like this movie," Clara says.

The kids are quiet during Jack and the Beanstalk until at

one point, Karen's phone lights up with a call from Mark. "It's Daddy," she says and Sam urges her to answer it. She whispers that they'll call him back when the movie is over. Later, during the animated song and dance finale, Sam complains that he has to pee. Of course he does; he finished the soda a half an hour ago. When Karen asks if he can wait, he says, "Okay," as if agreeing to clean up his toys.

She stands as soon as she sees the credits and carries Sam back up the stairs to the lobby exit. The doors are locked and an usher stands in front of them. He points to another door to the left of the screen. "My son really has to go to the bathroom," she says.

"I'm sorry," says the usher, and points again to the other exit.

She grabs Clara's hand and they return down the carpeted stairs. The exit leaves them in the middle of the mall. "I have to go now," Sam says.

"I know you do." She glances around but finds no sign directing her to a restroom. She rebalances Sam on her hip and says to Clara, "We've got to run." They do; Clara struggles to keep up. They pass the clothing vendors and coffee stands in the center of the hall and run towards the arcade, once again overwhelmed by the volume of game sounds.

"Momma!" Sam shouts. "I can't!"

"Just try," she shouts back.

"I can't! It hurts!" Then he begins to scream.

She thrusts her son in front of her as urine streams down his pants, drips over his shoes and onto the floor. "I peed!" he screams, and now he's crying as if he's been shot by one of the blasts thundering from a game. A sign for the women's bathroom points them down a long florescent hallway. Sam's screaming echoes through it. He's crying so hard that Karen can't understand what he's saying.

Clara bursts into the bathroom, nearly knocking over a

woman behind the door, and disappears into one of the stalls. Karen places Sam on the sink and tries to take off his sandals, but he kicks at her.

A teenage girl comes out from one of the stalls and stands behind Karen. She's maybe fifteen or sixteen years old with tired eyes and is so boney that Karen can almost hear her arm snap under pressure. Her blue jeans, probably size seven in children's, wrap tightly around her legs, and the pink kitten printed on the front of her t-shirt is faded nearly out of recognition. This girl watches Sam through the mirror. Meanwhile, Sam is still screaming.

Karen takes her sopping son into the stall next to Clara's. Standing on a toilet, he starts to calm down. He's still crying, still announcing that he's peed, but no longer screaming or kicking. He lets Karen tug off his jeans. She looks around for toilet paper and remembers that she has to buy it from a vending machine near the sink. A box costs five baht.

The girl in the kitten shirt is still there when Karen leaves the stall. She steps out of the way as Karen returns her son to the sink. The faucet has a hand-sensor. She puts her purse on the counter and tells Sam to crouch down beneath the tap. He does and yells at the girl staring at them, "Go away!" He's scrunching his face and glaring at them through the mirror reflection. From her lack of reactions, she can't understand him.

"It's okay," Karen says to Sam. "We're almost done." She waves her hand beneath the faucet to keep it running.

Another women emerges from a stall at the other end of the bathroom, older, well-dressed in a maroon pant suit, perhaps someone who works at the mall. She eyes the girl in the kitten shirt and eyes Karen. Meanwhile, there's no paper towel; only an air dryer.

The girl moves next to Karen and laughs at Sam's legs beneath the hot air. "Please step back," Karen says to her, glancing at the other woman in desperation. "You've embarrassed him enough already." The girl smiles. The suited woman says something in Thai to the girl, who makes no indication—no smile, no eyebrows twitching, nothing—that she's heard the woman.

Karen smiles and shakes her head as she rinses Sam's sandals. He protests when she tries to return the soggy leather to his feet. Again, he starts to cry and the same girl approaches him as if to comfort him. She puts the back of her hand on his cheek. Sam tries to bite her fingers.

"Don't," Karen says, and to the girl, "Please, stop."

She laughs again and puts her hand on the back of Sam's neck.

"He doesn't want you to touch him," Karen says, this time sounding angry, but the girl just stands there and ruffles Sam's hair. Sam screams. The woman in the suit grabs her purse from the sink next to Karen's, and rushes through the door. In the same instant, Karen places her palm on the girl's chest, shoving her away harder than she intended. The girl stumbles back.

The door is still swinging from the woman's exit. Sam is still screaming. Two more women shuffle into the bathroom, but Karen can't look at them. The girl, now backed up against a stall, stares at Karen as if she's waiting for her to say something, or as if she's considering how to fight back.

Karen is just about to call for Clara when her daughter wraps her arms around her leg and buries her face into the back of her knee. Karen lifts Sam to her hip, the movement alerting her to how much her stomach hurts. Too much popcorn followed by too much action. She clutches Sam tighter. The feel of his warm belly against the skin of her arm calms her a bit, and she closes her eyes. She opens them when the woman in the maroon suits bursts into the bathroom, accompanied by a female security officer.

"She grabbed me," Sam yells and points to the girl who has

not yet moved. "She doesn't understand English!"   She's slumped against the stall in alarm or shame or both.

The security officer offers no indication that she can understand Sam and says something to the girl in Thai. She follows the officer into the hallway, and now Karen is alone in the bathroom with her children. She knows she should go after the officer, but how can she word what happened in a way they'll understand? She lists all the Thai words she knows: foreigner, hello, bird, pig, and what animal did Gwang say her name meant? And how do Thai people say good-bye? Is it possible that she's been here a week and still doesn't know how to say good-bye?

On her way to the exit, her phone buzzes, shaking in her purse on the sink counter. She inhales at her small fortune in the coincidence, knowing that in all the commotion, she would have left it there and created more commotion. As she slings it over her shoulder, it stops buzzing. She figure's it's Mark and she doesn't want to explain what happened in here; she doesn't want hear her voice echo anymore among these stalls. She shifts Sam higher on to her hip and nods at Clara to get the bathroom door. The hallways are clear.

To her left, there is an elevator but the map beside it is completely in Thai. She steps back, for a moment imagining that if she could comprehend the bubbly script, she would follow the lines and curves to the security office, sweep through the door, and rattle off in perfect Thai that there has been a misunderstanding. I'm sorry, she'd say: *kor tot ka*. It's a phrase that Gwang taught her, a phrase she remembers is literally translated: punish me. This girl has done nothing, she'd say. Let her go. She'd ask the girl if she was all right. They'd leave the office. This is my son Sam, she'd say. This is my daughter, Clara. They'd walk together to the taxi queue, and Karen would offer to pay for her ride. She had no idea whether this girl would accept.

The thought that she cannot do this weighs her back into

the wall, and she shifts her son in front of her. Clara reaches for the down button on the elevator, but Karen stops her with something between a growl and a grunt, something from before there was language.

Her purse buzzes again. She'll have to explain to Mark that, no, they haven't eaten dinner yet because they were watching a movie, and no, they did not have a good time. But after that, she has no idea what to tell him. She cannot explain: They just won't leave Sam alone. She can't say this, knowing that by "they" she'd mean every last woman in Thailand, and knowing that referring to Thai people as "they" was something she and Mark agreed they would never do—especially not in front of their children.

She digs out her phone and its flashing numbers indicate that the call is not from Mark, but from a number she does not recognize. She doesn't know how to say "wrong number." She doesn't know how to say "sorry." Below the alert, the time reads 3:47 p.m. In Detroit she'd still be sleeping, hours before she'd have to wake up.

SLEEPING BEAUTY

AYDIN M. AKGÜN

In this tower of glass and steel, surrounded
by a forest of cables, IVs and tubes that hang
like thorn covered vines around her bed,
she sleeps, endlessly trapped in morphine dreams.
It took one prick to bring her here, one prick,
one vial of blood, two or three oncologists,
a scan, a biopsy, a spreading mass of thick,
maleficently silent fibrous strands.

Her husband, that poor, sweet prince, visits
between his shifts, and talks about his day,
the children, how she will wake up, rejoin
all those who love her. And each night, before
he leaves, he runs his hands through her brass
colored wig, touches her deathly pale face,
and leans in nervously like a boy of sixteen,
who still believes in true love's kiss.

SNOW WHITE

Aydın M. Akgün

Does the once-fair girl in white
walking down to the CT room
think of mirrors when they slide
her into that coffin-of-a-scanner
that reveals more than glass?

Or does she think of her admirers:
the short doctor, the sleepy nurse,
the grumpy PA, the dopey orderly,
the sneezy resident, the happy
volunteer or the bashful priest?

She answers my questions without
a single word, raising her hand
to touch the bite-size lump
lodged in her swollen pale throat.

YEAR OF HIDING OUT

Jana-Lee Germaine

I slept in damp bedclothes, ceaseless
snip snip of water off the eaves.
The rain, unending. Ink bleeding into paper.

Then fog exhaled over beaches,
breathing up and down stone stairs
cut into the cliff wall,
and I could walk the canal
or not walk, and the world
looked the same. I lived inside
the grey lung of a whale
where everything I touched spat
He would find me. He would not.

The walls grew a skin of moss,
carpet like a wrung sponge.
Black mold crept up the backs of doors.
In the closet, my shoes sprouted
mushrooms, blind, bulbous things
on slender stems. They surprised
my fingers with cool silk
when I reached for a pair of slippers.

Night and day were two hands
on the same body.
I walked circles through the house,
touching wood at every turn:
cherry sideboard, hickory bowl.
He will find me. He will not.

Unseen in fog, grebes chirked and screaked.
Everything searches for something
that doesn't want to be found.
Splashes in the canal. Cormorants, I thought.
Egrets. Ducks.

If I could leave
this world, I'd swim
a straight line past the herring gulls

until he and I were parallel
strokes of the letter H, certain
never to touch.

INTO THE LAKE

Lynn Gordon

Jim Buckley was fifty-five years old and he felt lucky to get a job at the Lake Valdez marina, even if it wasn't a position behind the register. Luke, it seemed, had a year's experience with fishing supplies and boat rental, so he was the one who told people what bait to use, got them to sign the paperwork, rang up the payments. Besides him there was Jonah, who handled the snack bar. He took in money but also made forays to the back room, where he'd rummage things out of the freezer and microwave them: Hot Pockets and crap like that. Customers gobbled the stuff up.

Anyway, Luke and Jonah, both about twenty or somewhere in there. All the kids had names like that now; you'd think the world was one big Bible. (It was true that his own name, Jim, was short for James and James was a saint, but you wouldn't hear the name Jim and have your mind fly straight to Christianity.) So those two, Luke and Jonah, had the choicer jobs, which left Jim hustling around the docks, handing out paddles and PFDs, helping people into the boats they'd rented, and unclipping the hawsers for them. Then of course when they came back from paddling or fishing, who but Jim was going to reverse the whole process. In between rentals he had maintenance, like bagging the garbage and sweeping.

Before this, only a few years earlier, he was the manager of a furniture store. The manager. He had people *under* him. The boss at the marina, Chuck Lansing, hardly came around and it was better when he didn't, but Jim had never been like him. Not when he was the boss.

He tried not to think about it, until one day a father and daughter came down the ramp to rent a kayak, and the daughter was in a chair. A wheelchair, with her feet twisted and her legs skinny and just not looking right. The father had gotten her to the dock by backing her down the ramp, but then he turned her around and smiled at Jim, saying, "A double." Meanwhile the girl was looking up at her father, sort of wiggling back and forth with happiness. Dressed in a long-sleeved pink shirt with her shorts, and Jim couldn't help thinking about Nance, a woman he'd hired at the store.

"Sure thing," said Jim. He wasn't going to act weird about the girl and her crippledness. He walked over to the newer one of the two doubles, a yellow plastic model that would wear like a battleship. No sense in anything but the safest. "Get yourself some life jackets from the bin."

The father leaned over the bin and straightened up with the jackets dangling from his hands. "One thing," he said. "The guy told me we could leave Molly's chair in your shed here on the dock."

Jim would take care of it, of course, but he didn't bother to answer. He laid boating cushions on the seats of the kayak— nothing special; that was standard—and then the father bent down to his daughter, tugged a little at the straps of her life jacket. In a graceful swoop he picked her up and settled her into the front seat of the kayak.

Once the yellow kayak had pulled away and was headed slowly up the lake, Jim unsnapped the brakes of the wheelchair, pushed the whole caboodle into the shed and left it. He walked to the end of the dock and stood watching the father and the girl windmilling their paddles, not really in synch, but he'd seen worse.

Molly—so that was her name. Not biblical. And she must be, what? Thirteen, fourteen. She turned her head and he saw her hair ruffle back, her face frown into the crosswind. Nance had had that frown when he gave her the news that she was hired, like she didn't want to show what a victory it was for her.

The two of them were acting about like usual, standing around and eating Slim Jims when they could have been working, peeling back the plastic wrappers. He set his forearm on the counter and fixed Luke in a stare, just for the roaring heck of it. "You check the insurance situation for that last rental? Seems to me it could be a problem." He jerked his head in the direction of the dock.

Luke took a bite of his Slim Jim and chewed it, gulped it down. "*Yes* we have insurance. Anyhow there's a waiver." Jonah was watching and grinning, a zit right at the corner of his mouth.

Luke closed his fist over his sausage wrapper and tossed it into a box behind the counter. "The geese are out there again," he said to Jim. "Don't you think you better get rid of them?"

A small lawn surrounded the building, and the geese always came around to graze. Sheep with feathers. Chuck Lansing had a thing about this; he wanted the geese kept off. If he'd had his way, he might have used a shotgun on them, but they were protected migratory birds and the most a person could legally do was to shoo them away.

Jim went up to the closest group, five or six of them wandering slowly around, bending their dark heads to the grass to eat. He could actually hear the ripping sound as they pulled up mouthfuls.

"Get!" he yelled. "Beat it!" They didn't scare easily. He whirled his arms around and that barely got their attention. He picked up a rag and waved it through the air. The nearest one settled down with its feet tucked under and grabbed a new mouthful of grass. Like it would stay forever.

Out on the water, the yellow kayak was moving further and further away, despite the bungle those two were making of their paddle stroke. As he stood, rag in hand, the kayak disappeared around a turn in the lake shore, leaving a furrow in the water behind it.

He had felt good hiring Nance. It's what he had tried to do as manager, give people a chance who maybe had something screwy about them. That was six or seven years back—say, 1988. Before the ADA came in, so he had to answer to the guys at the Central Office. Well, it wasn't *around* 1988; it was that year exactly and he knew it.

So she came in, a little chubby with strawberry blond hair in a heavy chair like armor. The maker's name, Everest and Jennings, stamped across the back.

"I don't have an opening," he'd said. "If you heard that, it was wrong."

"I just came in to introduce myself." She wasn't frowning then; she was smiling with her mouth a little to one side, like she would have laughed except it wouldn't be smart. "I can sell," she said. "That's why I'm here. Before this I was in housewares, at The Chopping Block." She opened a folder on her lap and handed him a typed resume. No crappy daisy-wheel, dot-matrix printing job—nice, clear, IBM typing. In her whole manner, a far cry from the likes of Luke and Jonah.

Something about the way she said *before this* made Jim think she meant before the wheelchair. She'd worked at the Chopping Block and then some accident or some disease had gotten to her.

"How many years of experience?" he asked. She looked about his own age, which was forty-eight at the time.

"Six years." He let that sit there, and after a moment she opened her eyes wider so they bored into him. "I'm good at it." She moved one of her feet; they were resting on a steel plate that was attached to the chair. She had on white leather sandals with nylons underneath, and one sandaled foot twitched over to the side, across the steel.

"Let me think it over," Jim said. "One of my people might be taking a vacation soon. You might be able to give it a try. Just temporary."

Not many people at the lake today: two families in pedal boats, plus the father and daughter in the kayak. A few fishermen along the shore; one in a pontoon boat. The water stretched in shimmers under a light breeze. Ducks and geese swam around here and there. One fisherman togged out in camouflage had fallen asleep in his chair in the sun.

The lake was a reservoir; somewhere in the eighteen hundreds they had dammed the Valdez River and let it fill up the canyon. Now, instead of running to the bay, the river was a big tank of drinking water. That meant boats only, no body contact, no swimming. On hot days, Jim had to tell little kids that they couldn't jump in.

He had slouched back in his office chair, a deluxe Steelcase with adjustable everything, and listened to Dwight from the Central Office.

"You have a new person selling now, a woman. I heard correctly, didn't I?" said Dwight.

"She's working out fine. You know what they say, plenty of women shop for furniture. They're making sixty percent of the decisions."

Dwight made throat-clearing noises. "We're a modern company, Jim. It's all right, it's even a *good* idea to have a woman sales hand." There was a pause during which Jim could picture Dwight behind his mahogany desk, using two fingers to part his thin mustache.

Jim didn't say anything, and Dwight came back at him again. "Look, we're a *furniture* store, stylish home furnishings. Think about our image. We don't want to give the impression that we're . . . orthopedic."

Jim tugged himself straight in his chair. "She did okay at the Chopping Block. I called over to the manager there and verified it." That was a lie. He hadn't checked a thing.

"Well you see, Jim, that's housewares," Dwight went on patiently. "Housewares are neutral. Women can use them standing up, sitting down, it doesn't matter what condition they're in."

That sounded reasonable to Jim until he thought about it. What kind of condition did people have to be in to use furniture? To lounge on a sofa, sit and eat dinner. Chrissake, to sleep in a bed even. "She just happens to sell like nobody's business. You'll be noticing, you watch."

Dwight was quiet for a while at his end. Then: "I'll let it go this once. But I'm expecting to see results."

He went around the side of the building and came back with a broom—not sure if that was legal or not. When he shouted and swung the broom, the geese began to move away, stepping limply with big, black feet. One opened its bill and brayed at him, showing a pink tongue.

Jim was watching his step; he had to. Those geese were turd machines beyond compare. He yelled some more, twitched the broom, and two more birds moved grudgingly toward the asphalt path.

The kayak had come back into sight, way at the far end; he could just make out the yellow, and the bits of pink that were Molly's sleeves. He took a step toward the lake for a better look. His foot went skidding over the grass.

As it turned out, Nance was nothing special at sales, just adequate, but he liked having her around anyhow—the way she'd roll over to him, frown and shake her head like he was a loser, but he could tell it was baloney. No matter what he said to her, she had a quick answer: "How you doing, Nance? You talk anyone into a living room set or two?" "Wish I could, but you know I don't like to show up the other floor staff. Leave it to me, I'll undersell them so they can feel good." He got sort of fascinated, too, at the way her head sat low on her shoulders. He was always wanting to bend down to see how she was joined together, see if he could get a glimpse of her neck through the strawberry hair.

She was fine to have around, but she had no big knack for sales. The one who did was Everett Burns, a younger guy Jim hired a year or two after Nance. Everett's hair stood up short and spiny over a narrow face; his nose probed forward. At the interview he wore a shirt with a stain on the pocket. He'd done six months for assault and battery, didn't sound like anything drastic, and Jim could tell he needed the work.

"I'll stake you to a new shirt," he'd said, and Everett said fine without even asking about the pay. From there he was off to the races. Surprisingly, he had the most rapport with old people. They seemed to like his old-timey haircut; they liked that his name was Everett. An older couple would come through the door and immediately Everett would take them in hand, ushering them to a corner of the store where the puffy lounge chairs stood out of view from the more fashionable customers.

"Try this out, ma'am," Everett would say to the women— always ladies first—and he'd touch the top of the chair back with one hand, swoop his other hand over the cushions so that no one could resist sitting down. "Lean back, that's it, and the footrest jumps right up for you. What do you think, you want to watch TV like this every night?"

Once they sank into the cushions, he had them. "This one's only $399, think of it—only one dollar a day for the first year, and after that it's free!" Pretty soon he'd be showing them the gliders, the models with power buttons and cup holders. Those old people would walk out of the store with a $699 item on order.

When Dwight called, which got to be hardly ever, he didn't talk any more about who was doing the selling. He complimented Jim on his store's profits, hinted about a bonus. Jim was smart enough to keep quiet about Everett's background. That was easier to keep secret than a blonde in a steel-plated chair.

A big cloud blew over the sun and dulled the sparkle of the lake. Leaves began to jiggle on the Chinese elms and eucalyptus trees, the way they did when rain was coming. Even though it was only October, it could rain. He went inside for his jacket.

"Still a lot of those geese out there," Luke said. He trickled the words out slowly.

"They live here." Jim punched an arm into his jacket sleeve. "What great works have you been accomplishing in here?"

A smile cut across Luke's face. "I heard Chuck Lansing's coming over. Jonah and I, we're both in good shape in here. Real good shape."

"You and me both," said Jim—exactly what Nance would have said. He snatched a bag of pretzel sticks from the shelves, pulled out a couple quarters and slid them over the counter, hard, so they clattered to the floor. *You and zit mouth*, he thought, just registering Jonah's look of surprise as he went stamping out the door.

The one time he and Nance went to Harvey's Stop-In for a sandwich, it was no big thing. Harvey's was practically next door, they just went over for some lunch because it was time and they were already talking.

"You ever take a vacation?" Nance had been asking. "In two years I've seen you here every day except Christmas. Maybe I should have come by on Christmas to check on you. Maybe you showed up, all by yourself."

"Yeah. You're not exactly gadding off to Palm Springs all the time." He felt bad for a second after he said that. He knew she lived with her brother's family, but that didn't mean it was easy for her to travel.

"I've been there." She took a big forkful of potato salad.

"Were you. What was it like?"

"Palm trees." One of them started laughing and then both of them. "Golf courses, swimming pools. Once was enough."

They both ate for a while. "How long ago?" Jim finally asked.

"Kind of long." Then, to his surprise, she came out with the answer to his unspoken question, the thing he'd been wondering about for months. "I have a condition, see." She was watching him—chewing her potato salad and holding her eyes on his face. "My bones like to break. So I don't want that happening while I'm out of town, with some doctor who doesn't know me." She poked at the last pickle slice on her plate, set her fork down. "Anyway."

"Yeah." He knew not to react. It would probably never come up again, but he'd heard what he'd heard. The knowledge made a quiver in his belly, down where an ulcer would be.

All the warmth had seeped out of the day. The surface of Lake Valdez was gray and restless, ripples forming in big chevrons across the water. The two families in pedal boats had turned back toward the dock. A man fishing from shore hefted his rod out of the sand and reeled in his line. Jim clumped down the ramp to the dock and positioned himself at the spot where the pedal boats would come in. The closer of the two, he could see, was the one with a couple little kids plus a baby that did nothing but sit on his mother's lap and drool. The older ones had started out raring to go, big red-lipped grins on them, but now they were fussing. One yelled that he was cold. The baby seemed to be crying. That happened a lot; kids liked the first five or ten minutes and then they'd had it.

He scanned out beyond the pedal boats for another glimpse of the yellow kayak, but saw only a pontoon boat parked on the gray water. Molly and her father must have slipped into the east-west arm at the far end

Jim got the pedal boats tied up and went back inside. "I'm taking my break," he told Luke. "If anybody wants to rent, you're in charge."

Jonah was watching. "They're not gonna want to. Look at the weather." He was chewing gum; the zit moved up and down.

Nance was having a banner day. A retired couple had come in—the kind of people who probably had arthritis and insomnia mixed together—bound and determined to get a new bed. It seemed the woman had laid down her cards: "If we're getting a new mattress, why not a frame, too. Something with a headboard; we've wanted that for years."

Afterward Nance had wheeled herself up to Jim's desk to tell him about it. "When we got to the Nordic model, the woman curled up on it and her husband got right down next to her. They were lying on it together, they rolled back and forth— who knew what would happen? Well, she gave him a big kiss." Nance giggled, unusual for her. "Then they got back up and looked at each other. That was it. Nightstands, too—the works."

Jim shook her hand. "A nice fat sale, just when I was ready to give up on you." He caught her eye then. "Only thing is, you're going to make the other staff feel second rate."

A gravel path ran along the west side of Lake Valdez. Jim hadn't walked it very often—normally he took his break standing around the parking lot or sitting in his car with a hot dog and maybe the radio on. Today was different. He was striding along the path, feeling the grit under his shoes, snatching looks at the lake through the trees.

Wind flooded through the branches and pushed at his face. He gouged his way into the bag of pretzels he'd bought, put three in his mouth at once.

Fifteen minutes gone already. He only had half an hour total. If he was late getting back, if Chuck Lansing witnessed that, Chuck was the kind of hard-ass who just might can him. It had happened before, he gathered. Chuck didn't give a crap what your story was.

The water was pushing across the lake now, bunching into waves. He could go faster on the way back, maybe jog a little, make up the time. All he wanted was to see that kayak. Make sure, that's all. You could say it was part of his job.

Those were the days when he still smoked, still took cigarette breaks. He'd gone out back—no smoking allowed in the showroom. He had the cigarette in his fingers, already lit as he pushed open the door. He closed his eyes to suck in the burning roughness that made everything else less burning, less rough. That first pull was the only good pull, really.

He opened his eyes to see Everett and Nance across the parking lot, yelling at each other. "I was doing my job, okay?" That was Nance.

"The fuck you were." Everett stooped forward, getting his nose in close to Nance's face. "You were stealing my customers, that's what you were doing. That's all there is to it."

Nance flipped the brakes on her chair and scooted backward

a foot or two. "Just because they're old people—"

"*I* take care of the old doddering people. Those are my customers. Ask anyone." Everett was getting louder, and Jim started toward him, to get him to shut up.

"—doesn't mean they're yours. And you were busy anyhow." Nance was holding her own.

"You going to fork over your commission? Are you? Because that's what you better do, I'm telling you." Everett ran his hand over his spiny hair in a way that looked like an obscene gesture.

"The *hell* you say." Nance was getting hoarse.

"Cut it out!" Jim called. Customers would hear; he started walking faster.

Everett ignored him. He began to roar. "You give me that money or I'll make you sorry. You give it!" He grabbed Nance's armrests and gave her a push backwards. Jim broke into a run; the cigarette fell from his hand. "You can't cut me out!" Everett went at Nance again, shoved her again. Jim was at a full trot and he saw it happening, Nance's hands out, her face furious, the chair tilting back and letting go. He saw her head hit.

There they were, finally. Twenty-five minutes into his break. The wind was behind them, driving them south, but the kayak kept turning crossways, wanting to nose into the wind. Molly had her paddle across her lap, probably tired. Water surged over the gunwales. Molly screamed as she got wet, just a tiny scream. The father was working his paddle, trying to get the kayak straightened out. Another wave swept into the cockpit.

Well, they'd manage. The wind would carry them back to the dock, just a matter of time. The kayak wouldn't swamp, would it? He'd never heard of that happening.

He turned around on the gravel trail, shook out a few more pretzels and shoved them into his mouth. Best to run. He couldn't run all the way, have to do what he could. Fly like a bat to make Chuck Lansing happy.

The pretzels snapped to pieces in his mouth and he swallowed them as he ran. He heard, over the shaking of the leaves, another little scream. He stopped, stumbled through the trees and down to the thin strip of sand that touched the water. Molly was holding her paddle now, her pink sleeves dark with water. She was okay, wasn't she? He tried waving and the father seemed to wave back with his paddle.

They had the kayak pointed south again. All right, then. Jim stuck the pretzel bag back in his pocket. In a few lunging steps he was back on the path and running again, then—gasping—petering down to a trot.

He hadn't gone far when the branches began to clatter on the trees. A sudden gust blasted him and he had to stop. He stood shivering, hands in his pockets, and felt the fabric pull tense against his knuckles. Suddenly again, the gale died back to a regular breeze.

Ah, one more look. That had been some wind, and it was getting cold, and they wouldn't have anything to bail with. He leaped down to the beach this time and caught himself with a few running steps. And there again the kayak, not so far, six or seven hundred feet if he had to guess, sideways again. The father good and wet, and Molly. Her hair that had blown free when they first set out, now lay dark and wet, sticking to her life jacket.

He thought of her chair, stowed away in the shed on the dock. He had placed it at a tidy angle, set the brakes, even passed a sponge over the seat that was already clean enough. Another wave sloshed into the kayak—a bigger one—and now, without thought or reason, he was leaving the sand beach and pitching himself into the lake, into the pent-up waters of the river trapped there for a hundred-some years.

The fierce October water invaded his clothes; it pulled and gripped him from all sides. It was getting deep quickly. The kayak was out ahead of him. He struggled forward, thinking he would start into a crawl stroke any moment, when his foot knocked against something far below the surface—probably the stump of a tree drowned long ago, a tree that had been vital and strong when the damming happened—and he was in to his neck before he caught himself, his fists splashing the waves.

He staggered up, his body tingling and full. Now the kayak was closer than before; he could get there. He would swim over the tree stumps of a century past, through all the cold water. The wind blew in a rush, and as he swam onward a picture rose within him—of two people kissing on a Nordic-model bed, surprising everyone.

THE MAKER

BRIAN LAIDLAW

for C.D. Wright

in the cold cabin with a rockhammer
striking snowflakes out
of your own breath, the goal being
to pound a breath so hard & so delicate
it turns into crystal forever.
Not many writers are makers
wheelwright shipwright wainwright
but the snowflakes conjoin
into mountains & map
a moraine below them, your breath
like a frozen shroud the earth pokes
up through, up beneath,
like the sheer clothing that makes a human
appear more naked:
more naked than naked.
A person can be a good ghost, even in life,
possessed by a grace so sheer
one's bodily angles protrude like snowcapped
pegasus-wings;
a person can be haunted by oneself
cartwright playwright ghostwright
such that death is a drawl that drawls on forever:
the valley of the unending vowel.

MOUNTAIN CLIMBING A RIVER

Michael T. Young

The Hudson anoints our summer reflections
in sun-flecked currents. My son,
pointing to the river says, "Why,
does the water have mountains on it?"

I could cut those peaks down for him,
break them into waves hoisted by wind,
but I rather his mind leap and dance
through wakes of Everests.

Later he could revise the nature
of the succulents by the bed, tell me
how the smell of their dirt fertilizes
my sleep from the windowsill,

what will take root in my dreaming brain,
sprout into a creeping vine, twining
a green embrace for the sky's orphans,
seed of what we are: questions

posing as answers. But I have aged
into the lustrous ache of this river,
a body of heavy churning, and wake
to the slowed currents of each morning,

blink sleep away, hope not to sink
before retrieving a small river stone
from the day's cloudy flux, something to offer
my son, or his sister when she asks,

"Why does it seem like everything
is going somewhere?" And I could give
the world back to her imagination, where
it belongs, rather than tell her, "Because it is."

INLET

David Frey

My father kept a little sailboat in the garage when I was young. It was a Sunfish, a narrow slipper of a boat, about as small as a sailboat could be, a Fiberglas dinghy with a single sail folded on top like an unused umbrella. It sat on a trailer wedged between my mother's Buick and the kids' bicycles.

The boat was one of the few hints I had of my father's life before I came to be. He was forty years old when I was born. As far as I could tell, he was born old.

But there was that black-and-white photograph of my father—the man who spent Saturday afternoons dozing on the couch while golf played on TV, who watched with my mother from the rail while my brother, sister and I loaded onto amusement park rides, who sat drinking Scotch with his business partner while I played cowboy alone at sunset—parasailing over the Acapulco beach. And there was that Sunfish he actually knew how to sail.

I saw him sail it only once. I was very small, too young for sailing. "This many," I would have said if you asked me my age, and held up three or four fingers. I sat on the beach with my mother while my father set off with my older brother and sister in a lake near our home in Central Pennsylvania. Their three figures hunched below the triangle sail. I contemplated the granules of sand on my toes. I can picture them still.

Apart from that one afternoon, the Sunfish sat unused in

the garage for years. Then one day it was gone. He sold it, I suppose, to someone whose dreams of freedom needed just a dinghy, a single sail, and a Saturday afternoon. Maybe it sat in his garage, too, unused. My father never mentioned the Sunfish after that.

My father was born in Germantown, Pennsylvania on the first day of summer in the last months before the Great Depression, and summer was the season he was most alive. My family spent as many weekends at the beach on the Jersey Shore as he could arrange, and as many weeks as he could spare from work. He bought a little condominium unit in an unglamorous seaside town called Sea Isle City, located on a narrow spit of an island separated from the mainland by a broad marsh. If we arrived at sunset, the whole waterway glowed orange and in its way could be just as beautiful as the ocean crashing on the other side.

He was a lawyer, and his vacations were as regimented as his workdays. He was the first to leave the apartment for the beach each morning, dressed for the day in a button-down beach shirt, a bathing suit, and an old pair of loafers. He set out with a book and a towel in one hand, a beach chair in the other and a big green umbrella over his shoulder, marched onto the sand to his estimation of the high tide mark and erected the wooden umbrella like a flag. Except for a brief walk, lunch, or a swim, he would remain there for the day until the sand was in the shadow of the high-rise condominiums or his round belly was red.

At first it was the five of us, my parents, my brother, my sister and I. Then my sister died. Non-Hodgkins lymphoma consumed her from the inside out so suddenly, she was dead almost as soon as we knew she was sick. She was fourteen and gone. Without her, the beach and everything else was never the same, but we went back, the four of us, to the beach and everything else. I was ten then. My brother was eighteen, starting college. In the years to come, he joined us less often at the beach, then not at all. Then we were just three.

A few miles to the south, toward the town of Avalon, our little island came to an end at a neck of water called Townsends Inlet, where the marshy waters flowed to the sea.

On the inland side of the inlet was a marina that rented boats. One weekend late in the summer when I was twelve, my father got the idea to rent a sailboat and explore thoroughfare, just he and I. We had never done anything like this before. We didn't have father-son outings. But my brother was off at college and my mother had no interest in leaving solid ground, so one morning, the two of us set off. We pushed away from the wooden dock in a little catamaran, a boat just slightly bigger than my dad's old Sunfish, with two fiberglass pontoons, a square of canvas between them, a single sail and a rudder. The boat etched a straight line across the channel, slid into the marsh grass in the shallows and came to a hissing halt.

"We'll have to get out and push," my father said. I protested. My body was lazy and warm in the sun on the canvas. The water was cold. I slid myself off the canvas and together, we stepped into the waters, sand oozing between our toes, the stalks of marsh grass jabbing like little knives. We set the boat free and hopped back aboard. The vessel slipped back across the channel, only to lodge itself in another mound of marsh grass on the other side.

"The rudder won't lock," my father said. He fought uselessly with the metal pole meant to steer us, but it wouldn't work. I couldn't say, then or now, if the problem was with the boat, or with my father's captaincy. It was clear, though, that if we couldn't control the boat, it would go wherever the wind and current took it. It was low tide. The current was drawing the water from the marshes into the inlet and out to sea. When we freed the boat from the marsh grass again, out to sea was exactly where it took us. The catamaran floated along the edge of the island, rounded the point and drifted toward the bridge that connected Sea Isle with the next island to the south.

The air cooled as we fell into the shadow of the bridge. My father wrestled with the rudder. It wouldn't budge.

The bottom of the bridge was angled so masted boats, like ours, could only pass at the narrowest point. I didn't know which would be better: to hit the bridge or pass beneath it, and I couldn't tell which we were going to do. The mast headed toward the narrow point but missed it by inches and struck the bridge with a clang. For a moment, we seemed to come to a stop. Then the current pulled us onward. The top of the mast stayed in place. The boat kept drifting, further and further under the bridge. We were like a problem in my school math book: a point, a straight line, a plane, and an arc drawn by the mast as it toppled behind us.

"We'll have to jump!" my father shouted. It was not the sort of thing I ever heard him say.

We leapt from the catamaran as it toppled upside down in the water behind us. My face went down in the green brine. When I emerged and blinked my eyes into focus, I saw we were floating out to sea, our orange life preservers around our necks like football players' shoulder pads. Our sailboat was still floating, upside down. My father swam to the boat and told me to do the same. I did. We heaved our chests onto a pontoon and together we rode the sailboat upended into the ocean, its sail sunk helplessly, its mast pointing at whatever lay below. Sharks, I imagined.

My father looked at me. His face glistened with seawater. "I'm sorry, David," he said.

I didn't need an apology. I loved him more at that moment

than I ever did before. I had never seen him try so hard. I know now he had tried so hard in so many ways I never saw.

Thankfully, passing boaters spotted us floating to our doom and called the Coast Guard. They motored up, took us on board their vessel, wrapped us in blankets and brought us back to the marina. One of them righted the catamaran and sailed it back solo, without any of the problems we had experienced. My father paid for whatever damage was done to the sailboat and we drove back to our condominium on the beach.

We arrived that afternoon to find my mother passed out drunk. She often was in the years after my sister died. She rarely drank before that, and rarely drinks now, but for a few years, she disappeared most afternoons into whatever comfort she found in whatever bottle she could locate. These were the waters my father usually had to navigate.

When I went to college six years later, I took a sailing class. An instructor took a small group of us out on a little lake in eastern Indiana on a little Sunfish. I learned about sailing windward in zigzag lines—tacking—to move forward against the gusts blowing against you; zigzagging leeward—jibing— to position the sails as you wanted them; and that moment when the boat points directly into the wind and the sail sags— luffing.

I learned the terms but never practiced them. The lake had no current and little wind. The sail mostly sat deflated: all luff, no jibe. We retreated to shore, folded down the mast, packed the Sunfish on the trailer and headed back to school. I never sailed again. My father was not a great sailor, but I would be no better.

That lesson offered a hint, though, of the unseen depths of knowledge my father had but never shared. As I grew older, greater depths slowly revealed themselves, but I would never see them all. Husband. Father. Soldier. Son. Businessman. Lawyer. I would only ever see a little of that man. When I became a stepfather to two boys, I would glimpse a little more of everything he had learned that I may never know.

RED SHIFT

Jed Myers

It was easy to seem eternal
not long ago—simple as teasing
our deaths just igniting each other's

cigarettes, that red-orange glow
and the river of taillights to deepen
the sunset, tinting us timeless . . .

Flushed with enticement, rosy
as newborns fresh from the womb of the past,
we were the present's flesh—

we undressed and undressed, our bloom
shaking loose in the gusts of our breaths,
soon down to the last

nakedness, all the world around us
vestige, drifts on drifts of the blood's
singed petals. Dusk was a rust

on the streets, the walls, the sheets . . .
And what was left of us? What had stood
from the first underneath—the stems,

now bared, thorned, near-leafless
and leaned in thirst. This is where
it begins. Real love, I mean.

WATERCOLOR

ANN QUINN

At home you will need something more . . .

—*Welcome Aboard: A Service Manual for the Naval Officer's Wife*

I can no longer see it, but when I was a child there was always
a smiling face in this picture. A sailboat is pulled up
    to the dock.
A   person   kneels,   elbows   on   the   gunwale,   speaking
with the sailor.

Both are simple stock fill-ins of people, the inverted triangle
of a torso, the brown strokes of legs. It was their hats, I think,
that looked to me like eyebrows on a smiling face. There is no

mastery here, it was from my mother's first and last
watercolor class, years before my birth. But the colors
are pleasing, the light blue of the water, and the way each

horizontal brushstroke resembles a wave. The sky
a different shade of blue, with purples and grays, and white
spaces left for clouds, the hills on the far
    shore rounded, womanly.

Now I see, those are the San Diego hills—she must have
painted this in Coronado, newly married, following the
    directive
of optimistic busy-ness for the new wife:

At home you will need something more than housework to keep
you occupied . . . take a course in a language, sewing, weaving,
pottery making, bridge. Of course!

She wasn't teaching, this tour was too short.
So she took a watercolor class on that cozy island
where my father rode to work on a scooter and was home

every evening. How I wish I could have lived there
        for a bit, but
my father's defection from Vietnam, but not the Navy,
        meant
no more ship duty for him, and we were sent East. Still,

I have this bright picture of the time before the war. I see
my mother's hand in the brushstrokes, her dark hair in
        the trunk
of the tree, her likeness in the birds vanishing into the
        California sky.

CANDIED KUMQUATS

Elaine Chiew

The new girl who comes to work at Candied Kumquats is from Central Asia. Somebody in this small rural town in Maine has given her the nickname Luanne, so Luanne is the name she comes with. She has another name, a name with deeper meaning, but no one can pronounce this or the name of the place she comes from.

The woman who runs the bakery pays the new girl less than the minimum wage. It's all she can afford, with the economy the way it is, the paper mills closing down, the winds heralding the coldest winter in ten years.

While his mother runs the mixers, the boy Hugo watches the new girl, apple-cheeked and bordering on plumpness, bending over the ovens. She ruffles his curls and tweaks his ear when she passes him. He twists his body away. He's eight and hates having his cheeks pinched. The new girl does not do that.

Winter touches down finally, every breath laden. Now the branches are draped with icicles. The air is dense. The boy finds it hard to breathe. He watches Luanne. He likes watching her because she's different. Magenta is her favorite color; she comes to work daily in this magenta smock that billows like bunting. Thick heavy furred boots, mittens shaped like oven mitts, hair plaited in two thick black ropes. The first week she arrived, she smelled like she'd been rolling around in hay or dog shit—it was all he could smell for days. But after a week, the aroma of the bakery overtook her. Now, to the boy, she smells just like candied kumquats and warm buttery croissants.

Her English sounds broken to him. She waves her hands about when she talks. Her words come haltingly to tell him she comes from a part of the world where the snow in winter lies like a blanket undisturbed except for the hooves of horses, but in the summer, the grass waves and the land is as dry as bone. The boy watches her dusting the cakes with icing sugar, her smock a tale of falling snow. Dressed-up berry, frosted fairy, he mimes. She laughs and ruffles his hair again. She tells him that in the evening she cries, she cries for home, but her tears are salt now, not ice.

He says he wouldn't like ever to be that far away from home.

She smiles. "One day you might. This my home now."

She tells him about the food she eats. Noodles and lamb skewers, red bean and shaved ice. One day she brings in a mangled mess of nuts and dried fruit and seeds, says 'matang'. The boy's mother tells her to take it out of the bakery.

The girl likes to hum under her breath. When she catches the boy looking at her, she hums in his ear, tickling the helix. He likes that too about her.

The idiot savant of the town is Ylapper. *Autisticvoyeuristicmajestic.* Ylapper can calculate exponential functions, watch balls fly in parabolas through the sky and calculate their precise speeds. He's called Ylapper because his words string together like a train wreck—*heavingheavinessbreathingbreathinessspinalelongation-medullablongata*—the words leaking air all over the place. His parents own the town's only shopping mall and a chain of stores all along Valhalla Way. The boy's mother leases the bakery from them, which is why Ylapper can come to the bakery anytime and ask for anything he wants.

So Ylapper comes into the bakery and says, *cuh.cuh.cuh.cuh. huh.huh.fuh.fuh*. His favorite cake is a genoise sponge cake, decorated with candied kumquats in sugar syrup.

The bell above the shop door tinkles. Ylapper stares at Luanne window-cleaning with a spray bottle and a paper towel. He follows the motions of her hands, clock-wise, round and round, with his hands. Ylapper's eyes drop. He watches the lifting of her armpit. The way her breasts move under the smock.

He blinks and his fingers splay in the air. He lifts his arm, twists his fingers into the shock of hair above his ear. He grins lopsided, and pushes his body forward.

"Evo!" he shouts. And scoops her breast into his palm.

The girl yells, Aydee! She sprays him with glass disinfectant. Ammonia fills the air. "Joo crazy bastard. Joo dirty fokker."

Ylapper clutches his nose, and then his mouth, where spray drops have landed. He begins to croon, shakes his head trance-like. *Ecstasyapostasythoughts of breast-larceny*. He babbles, fingers through his hair, raising the ends into a coxcomb. Then, he brings his hands together, clasping them, as if to pray, and begins to vibrate from side to side.

Hugo runs and hides behind the curtain separating the bakery from the kitchen. Luanne runs behind the counter, grabs a metal teaspoon, circles back out and efficiently raps Ylapper on the head. Ylapper clutches his head, shakes and shakes. He continues babbling. One word in this torrent sticks out. *Luanne*.

Ylapper blows raspberries. Pointer finger thrumming his lips. Then, as slowly as he can, he enunciates, *Vy like ev.eh*.

"Joo moron," the girl spits.

He wrings one hand. With one finger, he reaches over and strokes Luanne's cheek. "Pretty."

Luanne shrieks, flaps both ends of her apron and disappears out the door, setting the bell tinkling. In blows a snap of frigid air, and Ylapper blunders past the door frame, whether in pursuit or escape nobody knows.

A policeman comes by the bakery several hours later. Tells Hugo's mom that Ylapper has been hospitalized with head injuries. "Girl claims he chased her and pulled her clothes off."

His mother looks everywhere but at the policeman. "Where is she now?"

"If it's what she claims it is, then she ought to go to the health clinic. There are procedures that need to be followed."

His mother frowns. "He is stronger than her. He's a lot stronger than people think."

"He isn't right in the head. And that's where she hits him. On the head."

"Is Ylapper okay?

"He's in the hospital. They have to do some kind of scan. That young man's parents. They're not too happy. They say she hit him with something really hard, like a brick, maybe." The police officer licks his pencil, one eyebrow rising, the meaning significant. "Thing is, nobody saw nothing. Could be a lover's quarrel. Parents say he's got a crush on the girl?"

Hugo's mother says nothing.

"You've never seen them inter . . . acting before this?" The policeman draws out the word 'interacting,' Hugo wonders why.

The mother glances down. She doesn't want any trouble at the bakery. It's been difficult enough with the mill closing, a husband needing hand-outs, the whole town full of men chilling their heels at home, and now this. She only took in the Asian girl because the Methodist minister came to ask for help. No one really knew how Luanne came to be in the town, some say a boatful of illegal immigrants, some say mail-order bride, some say look at her eyes that follow you down the road.

"Didn't nobody see anything?" The policeman leans his

elbow on the counter, looking at the croissants and fruit tarts and pinwheel cookies.

His mother busies herself arranging madeleines on a tray.

"She ran out like nobody's business, out in the street for all to see. I would've thought somebody saw something."

"Well, I don't know anything. This boy . . . Floyd . . . he comes in for cake. That's all. It's not my business to keep tabs on my employees." The mother pauses, then says, "She's a grown-up, she's free to do as she likes."

"Ok, ma'am, just doing my job." He licks his pencil again and writes in his notebook. Then he looks down at the boy; the police officer's brow is like an Etch-A-Sketch of a flowing river. "You know anything, boy? You look like you got eyes big as a deer, you musta seen something."

Hugo looks at the officer, looks at the pencil and the notebook waiting in his hand, looks up at his mother. He shakes his head, trembling as he does so.

The policeman grabs a piece of madeleine on his way out.

Luanne returns to work. The boy watches her closely. She sits outside on a stone bench during her breaks. Amidst the bowl of snow and icicles she's the magenta ice queen. Huddled in her padded jacket, she throws frozen twigs at other people's dogs, hitting them. When she comes back in, her hands are chapped and her face is blue, but she doesn't warm herself near the ovens like she used to. Her hands shake when arranging muffins and banana cake and sometimes she breaks things. She no longer ruffles his hair or tweaks his ears.

"Did Luanne do something?" Hugo asks his mother one night.

His mother continues with her sewing. "I suppose they'll have to send her home." She strokes his hair and tells him to go to sleep.

A thought occurs to him. "She won't have to go to jail, will she?"

"I don't rightly know. It depends on whether Ylapper's parents decide to press charges. Now go to sleep."

"I like Luanne."

His mother doesn't reply.

"She tells me about her home place. She says it's full of mountains where she's from. She says it's cold and dry and windy there."

His mother bites off the bit of string after tying a knot. "Go to sleep, mind your own business."

"Mom, what does it mean, inter . . . acting?" He mimics the way the police officer has pronounced the word.

The mother is silent for a spell.

"Mom?"

"You ask too many questions, sweet. Hush now or you'll have bad dreams."

Even though his eyes are closed, his eyelashes are flickering.

"She didn't do nothing wrong."

The mother's hand stops stroking his hair.

"Anything. She didn't do anything wrong."

Hugo settles into silence. He's told *it* now. His chest relaxes.

His mother's tone changes. Becomes urgent, whispery. "Did you see something that day the officer came? Did you see Luanne hitting him?"

Hugo's eyes remain closed. He isn't in the least sleepy. "He was doing something naughty."

"What's that? What did you see?" Hugo thinks about that day, Ylapper grabbing for Luanne. Pinpricks in his eyes. He can feel his mother listening. Then, she resumes stroking his head. "You saw her hitting him, didn't you?"

He feels confused. He did see Luanne take hold of the metal

spoon. She had called Ylapper some bad words. She had sprayed him with cleaning detergent. She had rapped him on the head with the spoon.

The mother leans down and gives him a kiss. "You saw her hitting him, didn't you? You did see that, didn't you?"

Commit a crime in America, America doesn't want you. Hugo overhears a customer in the bakery saying this.

There's a trial. His father comes all the way from the next town where he now lives with a young woman who works as a waitress. His father will take him to the trial because his mother has to mind the bakery.

Hugo remembers the big man who spoke to him two days ago. His name is Mr. Stevens but he tells him to call him Mr. Prosecutor. He has meaty fingers, a signet ring choking the pinkie. He said boy, there's nothing to be afraid of, speak loudly and clearly, the judge and the prosecution are on your side. Tell only the truth and nothing else. The truth he'd told the officer at the station: what he'd seen, how Luanne sprayed and hit Ylapper with a metal spoon; how she'd screamed filthy words at him, and then run away.

We're a family that lives by the truth, his mother had said. She'd worn her Sunday best and put lipstick on. A button was missing from the dress, and through its crevice he could I-spy a patch of her lacy 'inner garment,' but he knew the dirty word for it. *Bra*. He'd pronounced the word in his mind, and a furtive feeling of pleasure crept over him.

Mr. Prosecutor was all smiles with her. "There's nothing to be worried about, ma'am. Just standard operating procedure. Trust the process. The truth will out."

He'd put his meaty fingers on his mother's back, and the gesture had irked Hugo. In a sudden flash of insight, he thought how Ylapper's hand on Luanne resembled the way Mr. Prosecutor was touching his mom. It wasn't where they touched, it was how. His dad had often told him, there were two things to being a gentleman. You always took off your hat if a woman passed by, and you never ever lay a finger on any woman unless she asked you to. But he hadn't told Mr. Prosecutor about Ylapper's hand. Mr. Prosecutor hadn't asked.

He looks up at his father now sitting beside him outside in the hall. The double oak doors to the court room are closed. He feels cold, sitting there in his buttoned-down Oxford shirt and thick woolen sweater. He fidgets, and his father puts a hand on his knee to stay him.

"They'll call for you in a minute. You know what to say, son?" His father's eyes have always reminded him of a frog's, bulging and green, but today they are watery and red-veined. Not as murky with drink. He nods and swallows.

"I'm proud of you, son. Takes a lot of courage to go up there before man and God and tell the truth and shame the devil. It's what separates a boy from a man."

"What's going to happen to Luanne, Dad?"

"I don't know all the ins and outs of it, son, but I suspect they will send her home."

The boy lowers his head, considering this. When the criminal charges were brought, the same policeman had come to the bakery and put handcuffs on Luanne. Hugo and his mother had watched silently. The event had drawn out half the town, standing outside in coats and parkas and mittens and snow boots.

"But she's in jail now."

"Only for a little while. Then they will send her home."

"But what if they don't? What if she doesn't want to go home?"

"I think that's the best place for her, don't you?"

The boy scratches behind his ear, there's a kind of hum in it. "But Ylapper is fine, isn't he? I saw him outside the bakery, wanting candied kumquats." The hum in his ear is louder, as if a gnat had gotten inside.

"That's not the point. She shouldn't have hit him like that. The boy is brain-damaged. He could've been seriously hurt."

"Dad, I saw Ylapper do a bad bad thing. He *touched* her."

Father and son are sitting side by side, without looking at each other, but the boy senses a sudden stillness in his father's posture. "Touch her where?"

Hugo demonstrates.

The father's eyes widen but he says, almost gruffly. "That isn't important."

Hugo shakes his head. "Why? Why isn't it important, Dad?"

"It isn't part of the story."

The boy hangs his head. "But I think she hit him because . . . "

"It isn't your job to think for the prosecutor, you got that? You tell what you told him the other day, and that's all. It isn't the time to be changing the story now."

The boy squirms. The undersides of his thighs are clammy with cold. His father is silent. Then he twists the boy's chin up to look at him.

"You tell the truth and nothing but the truth. Didn't your mother and I always tell you we're a family that tells the truth?"

When the boy walks down between the benches of the courtroom, the eyes on him remind him of a colony of seals in his animal picture book. There are Ylapper's parents, seated up front. Ylapper's father gives him an encouraging nod; Ylapper's mother smiles at him, and the boy sees that she has lipstick on her teeth. But Ylapper himself is not there.

The boy steps up to the stand. The bailiff instructs him to put his hand on the Bible and repeat after him. The boy screws his head round to look for his father but can't locate him amidst the dozens of heads. Instead, he sees Luanne, seated next to a sallow man in a wool suit. In a sea of brown, black and gray, she's the only one ruched as bright as a bird, in her yellow padded jacket, her black braids adorned with magenta ribbons. As if she's going to the fair or circus, a joyous event.

Two red welts on her chin. Her nostrils flare when his gaze locks onto hers. The boy feels a tremor begin to seize him, travelling up from his ankles to the shin-bone to the thigh-bone.

The prosecutor smiles. The boy looks away.

The prosecutor is telling him not to be afraid, to state his name and age for the record. Gently, he leads the way, a shepherd guiding one lost sheep.

The boy's voice comes out as whispery as a blown leaf, but he keeps his eyes level with the prosecutor's. He answers questions about school and play, about Ylapper coming to the bakery. The prosecutor interrupts to announce something for the record, and the boy understands it's to identify Ylapper's real name. Floyd. Floyd Weaver.

The boy sees it's like a story. How the prosecutor is setting it up so everyone can understand it better. Now they come to the part of how Ylapper came in that day and Luanne sprayed him with window disinfectant.

The boy hesitates, disoriented; he looks for his father. He sees dots of colour that pose as eyes, bits and pieces of ears and mouths and nose, bits that refuse to assemble into faces. His eyes pan the benches in wide anxiety. The prosecutor calls his attention.

"I saw Ylapper . . . " The boy clears his throat.

"Floyd," the prosecutor corrects.

"Floyd. Floyd was acting weird and she sprayed him with the window-cleaning bottle. There was liquid in it."

"And by she, I take it you mean the defendant?" The

prosecutor pointed his thumb at Luanne. The boy nods.

"And how did he react to this? Did she spray him in the eye?"

"Objection. Leading." The sallow man has suddenly risen and spoken. The boy blinks.

"Let me rephrase. How did she spray him?"

"I don't remember," the boy says. "He was acting weird and she sprayed him, that's all."

"She also hit him with a metal spoon unprovoked, did she not?"

"Objection."

"Sustained."

"Let's rewind. You say he's acting weird? How exactly?"

"The way he always does. Rocking. Talking words that make no sense. Like dressed-up berry, frosted fairy."

There was a sound like rustled laughter, the prosecutor frowns. "Is that all? Did he say anything to her before she sprayed him?"

The boy shakes his head.

"You need to answer yes or no."

"No."

"Tell us what happened next."

"Wait." The boy pauses. The trembling is making him feel ill. The prosecutor's eyes regard him. They didn't go through this part in this much detail two days ago.

"Yes?"

"He was staring at her. He always stares at her."

"Ylapper . . . I mean Floyd Weaver was staring. Was there anything else?"

"He was standing real close to her."

"Was that all? Just standing close?"

The boy opens his mouth and nothing comes out. An urge tickling his throat. He looks up. It's then he sees his father, standing at the very back. His father shaking his head. The boy's face suddenly feels funny to him—too hot, as if little needles are stinging him, a mirror of Luanne's bright cheeks, her eyes glowing like live coals. The boy lifts the hand that does not want to be on his knee, unsure of where to put it. Then he puts it underneath his armpit and lets it travel to his chest, lets it scoop.

The sallow man at Luanne's side rises, saying something about stipulated facts. The boy hears the words 'metallic spoon' and 'rap over the head.' The prosecutor replies, the court stenographer stops typing, and everyone looks at the judge. The boy understands none of it.

"Is there anything else you'd like to add, Hugo?" But the prosecutor's tone is different now. A kind of triumph in it, or a quiet satisfaction. The way his mother sounds when she counts the money in the register at the end of the day.

The boy swallows. A violent hum in his ear; he can't hear anything but the hum. He doesn't hear himself uttering yes, then no, the prosecutor asking him which is it. The boy's gaze turns filmy, like a veil being passed to shutter his sight. His eyes, ears and nose no longer belonging to him. He doesn't know the word they're after, but the word he seeks hovers just barely out of reach, *touch*, the word that ever after, he'll spend his life revisiting, the word that separates the boy from, not the man he inexorably becomes, but the other boy, Hugo, the boy he really is.

TRIBAL BEAUTY, UGANDA

Marsha Mathews

Lugbara
At puberty, patterns of dots are cut
near her mouth, across her forehead,
her waist.

Such beauty will bring men
all the way
from Mount Wati.

And her nose, if pierced
with a jewel or shell,
a goddess.

Banyarwanda
If only she is gracious.
If she is curvy.
If her skin is dark as cacao.
If her teeth are whiter than cowries.
If she has a long straight neck
adorned with beads
and gums dark as a no-moon night.

Bakiga
Best are those with thick bodies,
strong and willing to work
both in the home and in the field.

She must carry herself
with poise.

A gap between her top front teeth,

most beautiful.

Karimojong
Here, a traditional woman proves her beauty
in a ceremonial fight.

She wears many beads, stones, and shells
around her neck, waist, arms, ankles.
Animal skins hang on her body.

She wrestles
the man who wants her
for his wife.

Two teeth of the lower jaw
knocked out—how desirable!

TRADITION

Amanda Hart Miller

Mahtab hurt but not in the way she should on a wedding night. And there was no blood. The sheets glowed under the moonlight, exposing her for what she had been since she was eleven: sullied. Bahram stood naked with his back to her, fists clenched, his muscles outlined by light and shadow. Beyond him, in the corner of the room, sat the child's rocking chair that they'd sat on throughout the years when they read the words of the Sufis and poets, the chair that they'd talked about giving to whatever children Allah might bless them with.

She sat on the floor with her knees hugged to her chest, the too-white bed on one side and their pile of mingled clothes on the other. Bahram would not be able to deliver the sheets to her parents, as was tradition, so she would become known as the whore who broke her marriage before it could even begin. Worse, this was Bahram, the boy she'd grown up with. He was the neighbor who would sneak to her dining room window to interrupt her solemn and boring meals with her parents by blowing glistening bubbles through the window, bubbles that would hover over their lamb and qorma, each impossible capsule of liquid quivering until Mahtab felt it might last forever. Then the bubbles would burst, droplets of soapy water falling into the meat and onions, and her too-serious father would cuss and close the window while her mother shook her head sadly. But Bahram would already be gone, his laughter and footsteps retreating down the street.

Those nights so long ago, after her mother and she cleaned the dishes, Mahtab would meet Bahram in the valley outside of town to race barefoot and laughing through the grass. He would tell her stories about his brave older brothers who were Jihad, how their honor was higher than the sun. "Not because they're fearless," Bahram explained proudly. "They're afraid, but they fight and do the hard things anyway, even when they don't want to." Of course, all that was before Bahram himself had killed anyone, when he was still getting used to the idea of it, when he was still a thin neighbor boy with brave older brothers.

This was her Bahram. This was who she'd disappointed. She had been hopeful that there would be blood tonight, maybe not as much blood as the first time the grocer's son Kaihaan had closed his hands around her neck and dragged her into the store's pantry five years ago. The blood gushed that day, and she had cried afterward, even wished for Bahram to be there to protect her, not caring then in her pain about the shame it would bring her if he saw her. But blood had also trickled from her later that year when Kaihaan trapped her in the alley behind Qasaba while she was on her way home from the school she used to attend, when she had hit him in the head with a rock but had failed to run away fast enough. Blood did not only accompany the first time, as her friend Asefa had told her long ago. It could also come when the man was angry, violent.

Bahram was not a man without rage. She'd seen it fester in him, as she mourned with him the deaths of his mother and brothers, as she pelted him with questions about the new Taliban regime, as she held him when he confessed to shooting a Talib on the road from Herat to Kabul. "A perfect forehead shot," he'd said, and she'd shivered at his lack of remorse. Each tragedy had stolen a piece of that boy she loved, and her theft tonight of yet another piece of him made her pray to Allah to have mercy on her, to have Bahram kill her.

When Bahram turned to her, she hid her face from him, looking between her fingers as he knelt to the pile of clothes. His face now housed scars, and age beyond his years. He drew his knife, its blade glinting in the moonlight. "Look at me, Mahtab."

She dropped her hands to her calves and squeezed her skin hard to summon bravery. Bahram stood over her, the knife in one hand, his other hand held toward her, palm facing her and fingers up and splayed, as if to warn her not to try to change his mind. He needn't worry about that. In some terrible place in her mind, she'd wanted this day to come. She was tired of pretending.

He brought the knife to his own palm, slowly, his eyes never leaving her, and pressed the tip into his flesh. She saw then that he was offering her what she'd been afraid to even hope for: his forgiveness of her for being raped.

The unfair, bitter gratitude of it all threatened to choke her. She rose, barefoot in the small bedroom, the clay ground cool like the blades of grass from the valley, and she grabbed the knife from him.

"My blood to give." She slashed her palm and then dragged it across the sheet. "My honor to prove. Not yours."

Bahram glared at her, and she wondered if his face had looked like this when he killed the Talib. Then he dropped his gaze to the bed and with his own bleeding hand he traced the smear of crimson. The scar on the right side of his chin crinkled as his lips rose in a smile. "Honor as high as the sun."

PHOTOGRAPH TAKEN BY AN EX-LOVER

Elizabeth Hazen

The question of the photograph concerns
your easy heart, the reckless optimism

that leads you to believe, with each new love,
This time will be different. The question

of the photograph is math that won't add up.
The answer cannot tell you who you are

or what you really want. You recognize
the lake, your son's hand in yours as you leap

together off the dock, bodies taut, bracing
for cold, caught mid-air by an invisible

finger's clicking. You remember your son's
sticky grip, his squeals, the way he reached for you

underwater. But the picture begs the question,
who was he who poised to snap and capture this

idyllic scene? Did he believe he could,
through preservation of this leap, preserve

his place with you? You remember the splash,
the shivering aftermath, but these details

change nothing. Who he was and what became
of him, the color of his eyes, his version

of the story, his version of who you are—
these answers are irrelevant. The echo

of broken promises holds no more meaning
than the faint chime of bells on a closing door.

People come and go. Most often no one
is at fault. We try and fail and try again.

We do the best we can. To the question of
the photograph you must simply reply:

My heart was open; I was not afraid.
I held my son's hand; I will not look back

AUTHOR BIOS

AYDIN M. AKGÜN was born and raised in Izmir, Turkey. He graduated from the Lycée Saint Joseph in Izmir and moved to the United States in 1995. He received his B.A. in both International Relations and French from the University of Nevada, Reno, in 2000, and his M.A. in Creative Writing in both poetry and fiction from Johns Hopkins University in 2009. Mr. Akgün lives and works in Washington, D.C. His poems have been published in the *Chicago Literary Review* and *Potomac Review*.

KILBY ALLEN received her Ph.D. from Florida State, where she was a Kingsbury Fellow in creative writing. She also holds an M.F.A. from Brooklyn College and was the Patricia McCorkle Scholar at the Sewanee Writers' Conference in 2014. Currently, she lives in Mississippi, where she teaches at Delta State University. Her work has appeared in *Nashville Review, Day One, Baltimore Review, CutBank, Potomac Review,* and elsewhere.

CARL AUERBACH has had three poems and a short story nominated for a Pushcart Prize. His work has appeared or is forthcoming in *Amarillo Bay, The Baltimore Review, Blue Lake Review, Brink Magazine, The Cape Rock, Colere, Confluence, Corium Magazine, descant, Evansville Review, Evening Street*

Review, Hawaii Pacific Review, Louisville Review, The MacGuffin, Nimrod International Journal, North American Review, Passager, Permafrost, Poem, RE:AL, Reed Magazine, Willow Review, and many other journals.

SUE HYON BAE is International Poetry Editor for *Hayden's Ferry Review*. Her work has appeared in *Four Chambers Press, Minetta Review, Apple Valley Review, Please Hold Magazine*, and elsewhere.

SHEILA BLACK is the author of *House of Bone* and *Love/Iraq* (CW Press, 2016) and *Wen Kroy*, which received the Orphic Prize in Poetry from Dream Horse Press. She co-edited with Jennifer Bartlett and Michael Northen, *Beauty is a Verb: The New Poetry of Disability*, from Cinco Puntos Press, named a 2012 Notable Book for Adults by the American Library Association. In 2012, she received a Witter Bynner Fellowship from the Library of Congress, for which she was selected by Philip Levine. She lives in San Antonio, Texas where she directs Gemini Ink, a literary arts center.

NORA BONNER is a Ph.D. student at Georgia State University in Creative Writing, Fiction. Her stories have appeared in *Shenandoah*, the *Bellingham Review*, *Juked*, the *North American Review*, *Hobart*, the *Indiana Review*, and the *Best American Non-Required Reading*. She is originally from Detroit.

BARBARA SIEGEL CARLSON is the author of *Fire Road* (Dream Horse Press, 2013) and co-translator of *Look Back, Look Ahead, Selected Poems of Sre ko Kosovel* (Ugly Duckling Presse, 2010). Her poetry and translations have appeared in *New Ohio Review, Prairie Schooner, Salamander, The Carolina Quarterly, Mid-American Review*, and others. She lives in Carver, MA.

ELAINE CHIEW is the editor of *Cooked Up: Food Fiction from Around the World* (New Internationalist, 2015). She won the 2008 Bridport Prize and the 2015 Elbow Prize. She's been published in numerous journals and anthologies, most recently in *Everything About Us* (Word Works, 2016) and *Singapore Love Stories* (Monsoon Books, 2016). She's currently pursuing a master's degree in Art History in Singapore.

ORMAN DAY's prose and poetry have been published by such journals as *Creative Nonfiction, ZYZZYVA, Third Coast, SLAB, William and Mary Review, Los Angeles Review,* and *Portland Review.*

RUTH FOLEY lives in Massachusetts, where she teaches English for Wheaton College. Her work has appeared in numerous web and print journals, including *Adroit, Sou'wester, Threepenny Review,* and *Valparaiso Poetry Review.* Her poems can also be found in several anthologies, including the *Best Indie Lit New England* anthology. She is the author of the chapbooks *Sink and Drift, Creature Feature,* and *Dear Turquoise,* and the forthcoming full-length collection *Dead Man's Float.* She serves as Managing Editor for *Cider Press Review.*

DAVID FREY is a freelance writer in Gaithersburg, Maryland. He holds a M.A. in Nonfiction Writing from Johns Hopkins University, and his work appears in a variety of publications, including the *San Francisco Chronicle, The Rumpus, Eater,* and *Narratively and Sunset Magazine.* He's a regular contributor to *Bethesda Magazine.*

JANA-LEE GERMAINE is a poet who received her M.F.A. from Emerson College. Although her home is in the Boston area, she is currently residing in the small village of Denton, England.

E. LAURA GOLBERG emigrated from England to America at age 21. Her poetry has appeared in *Birmingham Poetry Review*, *RHINO*, *Gargoyle*, *Pebble Lake Review* and the *Journal of Humanistic Mathematics*, among other places. Laura won first place in the DC Commission on the Arts Larry Neal Poetry Competition.

LYNN GORDON'S fiction has appeared in *Baltimore Review*, *Epiphany*, *The Southampton Review*, *Zone 3*, and other magazines. Lynn lives in Northern California.

JEFF HARDIN is the author of *Fall Sanctuary*, recipient of the Nicholas Roerich Prize, and *Notes for a Praise Book*, selected by Toi Derricotte for the Jacar Press Book Award. His third collection, *Restoring the Narrative*, received the 2015 Donald Justice Poetry from West Chester University Poetry Center. His fourth collection, *Small Revolution*, appeared in early 2016. His poems have been published in *The New Republic*, *The Hudson Review*, *The Southern Review*, *Southwest Review*, *North American Review*, *The Gettysburg Review*, *Poetry Northwest*, and elsewhere. He teaches at Columbia State Community College in Columbia, TN.

ELIZABETH HAZEN is a poet and essayist whose work has appeared in *Best American Poetry 2013*, *The Normal*

School, Southwest Review, The Threepenny Review, and other journals. Her debut poetry collection, *Chaos Theories*, was published in April 2016. She teaches English at Calvert School in Baltimore.

PHIL HEARN is a fiction and freelance writer based in Baltimore. His work has appeared in *Post Road Magazine*, and he has been nominated for the Pushcart Prize.

SHERRI H. HOFFMAN holds an M.F.A. from Pacific University and is currently a Ph.D. candidate at the University of Wisconsin-Milwaukee in Creative Writing. Selected publications include *december, PANK, Etchings, Delmarva Review* and forthcoming in *Cimarron Review*. She is a co-editor of *Utah Reflections: Stories from the Wasatch Front* and is currently a fiction editor at *Cream City Review*.

FAITH S. HOLSAERT co-edited *Hands on the Freedom Plow: Personal Accounts by Women in SNCC*. She was awarded the 2013 Press 53 Open Awards in the novella. She received her M.F.A. from the Warren Wilson Program for Writers.

DOUGLAS S. JONES holds an M.F.A. from Arizona State University and is the author of the chapbook *No Turning East*. His poems have appeared in *The Pinch, Blackbird, Barrow Street, Sentence: A Journal of Literary Poetics*, and elsewhere, and have been featured in *American Life in Poetry*. In 2006 he participated in Poesía del Sol, a program that brought poetry into the rooms of palliative care patients at the Mayo Clinic. That year, the program was awarded the Arizona Governor's Arts Award. He also served as Poet in Residence at St. Chad's College at the University of Durham, England. Currently, Jones teaches at Western State Colorado University.

BRIAN LAIDLAW is a poet from San Francisco, now based in Minneapolis. His work has appeared in *Agni*, *Field*, *New American Writing*, *The Iowa Review*, *American Songwriter* and dozens of other publications, and was also included in The Arcadia Project anthology from Ahsahta Press. His first full-length book of poems, *The Stuntman*, was just published by Milkweed Editions.

LYN LIFSHIN has published over 130 chapbooks, including 3 from Black Sparrow Press: *Cold Comfort*, *Before It's Light*, and *Another Woman Who Looks Like Me*. Before *Secretariat: The Red Freak, The Miracle*, Lifshin published her prize winning book about the short lived beautiful race horse Ruffian, *The Licorice Daughter: My Year With Ruffian* and *Barbaro: Beyond Brokeness*. Recent books include *Ballroom*, *All The Poets Who Have Touched Me*, *Living And Dead*, *All True, Especially The Lies*. NYQ Books published *A Girl Goes Into The Woods*. Also just out: *For The Roses: Poems Inspired By Joni Mitchell* and *Hotel Hitchcock* from Danse Macabre.

MARSHA MATHEWS is an American writer, a graduate of both University of Florida and Florida State University, and is currently a Professor of English at Dalton State College, in Dalton, Georgia. Her fourth chapbook, *Growing Up with Pigtails*, has just been released by Aldrich Press. Marsha's writing has appeared in literary journals, such as *Fourth River*, *Greensboro Review*, *The Los Angeles Review*, *Pembroke*, *Raleigh Review*, and in numerous anthologies. Marsha received the Orlando Prize for Flash Fiction.

AMANDA HART MILLER holds a Master of Arts in Writing from Johns Hopkins University and she teaches composition, literature, and creative writing at a community college in Maryland. Her fiction and poetry have appeared in nearly twenty literary magazines, including *PANK*, *Literary Mama*, *Apeiron Review*, and *Scissors & Spackle*. Her short story "Inventory" won June 2014 Story of the Month at *Bartleby Snopes* and her story "Pansy" was nominated for a 2013 Pushcart Prize. She has also published several children's books.

JED MYERS lives in Seattle. His poetry collections include *Watching the Perseids*, which won the Sacramento Poetry Center Book Award, the chapbook *The Nameless* from Finishing Line Press, and a chapbook forthcoming from Egress Studio Press. His work has received Southern Indiana Review's Editors' Award, the Literal Latte Poetry Award, *Blue Lyra Review's* Longish Poem Award, and, in the UK, the McLellan Poetry Prize. His poems have appeared in *Prairie Schooner*, *Nimrod*, *Harpur Palate*, *Crab Creek Review*, *Cider Press Review*, *Painted Bride Quarterly*, and elsewhere. He has recently been guest Poetry Editor for the journal Bracken.

BIBHU PADHI has published ten books of poetry. His poems have appeared in magazines throughout the English-speaking world, such as *Contemporary Review*, *The Poetry Review*, *Confrontation*, *New Letters*, *Poet Lore*, *Prairie Schooner*, *Poetry* (Chicago), *Southwest Review*, *Tulane Review*, *The New Criterion*, *Rosebud*, *TriQuarterly*, *Antigonish Review*, *The Illustrated Weekly of India and Indian Literature*. His poems have been included in numerous anthologies and textbooks; three of the most recent are *Language for a New Century*, *60 Indian Poets*, and *The HarperCollins Book of English Poetry*.

ANN QUINN lives in Catonsville, Maryland. She teaches clarinet and writing and plays clarinet with the Columbia Orchestra. She won first prize in the 2015 Bethesda Literary Festival Poetry Contest, judged by Stanley Plumly, and has been nominated for a Pushcart Prize. Her poems have appeared in *Little Patuxent Review*, *Beechwood Review*, *Haibun Today*, and *Snapdragon Journal*. She is working towards an M.F.A. in poetry at the Rainier Writing Workshop of Pacific Lutheran University.

CHAD SCHUSTER'S fiction has appeared or is forthcoming in *Glimmer Train*, *Hobart*, *Gulf Stream*, *Barrelhouse* and elsewhere. He lives near Seattle with his wife and two children.

MARK SENKUS lives in Michigan's Upper Peninsula and works as a psychotherapist. He has appeared in *Chiron Review*, *Pif Magazine*, *Miller's Pond*, and *Rattle Poetry Journal*. He was widely published in the small press poetry underground of the late 1990s. He recently began writing again after a twelve year hiatus from poetry.

JOHN L. STANIZZI is the author of *Ecstasy Among Ghosts*, *Sleepwalking*, *Dance Against the Wall*, *After the Bell*, and *Hallelujah Time!* His poems have appeared in *Prairie Schooner*, *American Life In Poetry*, *Chiron Review*, *Tar River Poetry*, *Rattle*, *Passages North*, *Poet Lore*, *Boston Literary Review*, and many other publications. His work has been featured on Garrison Keillor's The Writer's Almanac. He is currently an adjunct professor of English at Manchester Community College. He lives with his wife in Coventry, Connecticut.

JAKE WEBER is a translator living in Maryland who volunteers as a mentor and English tutor for refugees from East Africa. He has an M.A. in English from University of Illinois at Chicago. He has published fiction in *The Baltimore Review* and *Bartleby Snopes*.

MICHELE WOLF is the author of two books: *Immersion, Conversations During Sleep*, and a chapbook: *The Keeper of Light* . In addition to *Potomac Review*, her poems have appeared in *Poetry, Boulevard, North American Review, Gargoyle, Southern Poetry Review*, and many other journals and anthologies, as well as on *Poetry Daily* and *Verse Daily*. Her work is forthcoming in *The Hudson Review* and two anthologies. She lives in Gaithersburg, Maryland and has served as a contributing editor for *Poet Lore* and taught at The Writer's Center.

SOPHIE WOLFRAM is a graduate student in Environmental Studies at the University of Montana. This is her first publication.

MICHAEL T. YOUNG's fourth collection, *The Beautiful Moment of Being Lost*, was published by Poets Wear Prada. His chapbook, *Living in the Counterpoint*, received the 2014 Jean Pedrick Award from the New England Poetry Club. He received a Fellowship from the New Jersey State Council on the Arts and the Chaffin Poetry Award. His work has appeared in numerous journals including *The Cortland Review, The Louisville Review, The Main Street Rag, Off the Coast*, and *Rattle*.

www.ingramcontent.com/pod-product-compliance
Lightning Source LLC
Chambersburg PA
CBHW032009170626
46807CB00006B/2722